NAUGHTY OR Ice

SYLVIA PIERCE

Naughty or Ice
Buffalo Tempest Hockey, Book One
Copyright © 2016 Sylvia Pierce
SylviaPierceBooks.com

Published by Two Gnomes Media

Cover design by Two Gnomes Media

v13

E-book ISBN: 978-1-948455-69-5
Paperback ISBN: 978-1-948455-01-5

ALSO BY SYLVIA PIERCE

BUFFALO TEMPEST HOCKEY

Naughty or Ice

Down to Puck

Big Hard Stick

BAD BOYS ON HOLIDAY

Bad Boy Valentine

Beached with the Bad Boy

Rescued by the Bad Boy

Bad Boy Summer

Bad Boys on the Beach: The Starfish Cove Collection

DEDICATION

For Janice Owen,
who's always on the nice list

CHAPTER ONE

The pain was damn near crippling.

Walker Dunn sucked in a breath of cold air and clenched his teeth, his skate trembling against the ice as he waited for the white-hot agony in his knee to subside. He hoped McKellen hadn't noticed.

Fuck.

That one had been bad. Stomach-churning bad. Seeing-stars bad.

But not bad enough for the once unstoppable Buffalo Tempest starting center to call it a day. Not until he'd nailed McKellen's agility drills. Walker had been working with the hockey trainer for over two months now—ever since the team doc had given the all-clear for practice again—and his times still weren't anywhere *near* where they'd been at the end of last season.

Shaking off the pain, Walker skated back to the goal line, signaled to McKellen to restart the stopwatch.

Three, two, one... and he was off, barreling toward McKellen and the orange cones at the other end of the rink. He'd ditched the stick and puck earlier, but he was otherwise geared up, the weight of his pads and helmet solid and familiar. The pain had finally dulled to a tolerable ache, and Walker pushed himself harder, faster, blades slashing across the ice, cold air whipping his face. He felt like a freight train, picking up speed with every powerful stroke.

Fuck yeah.

He was past center ice and closing in on the cones.

Fifty feet, forty.

The knee would hold up this time.

Twenty-five feet.

Had to.

Ten. Five. Two, and *boom.*

The cones were an orange blur as Walker cut his blades and swizzled around the first set, his turns tight, muscles limber as he plowed through the course.

"That's it, forty-six," McKellen called out. "Keep it going!"

Whipping around behind the net, Walker tore down the rink to his starting position, then looped back to the cones for another go. Again. Again. Each time feeling stronger, faster, more powerful. The ache in his knee was a distant memory as his muscles and bones and heart and fucking soul all lined up to do what they did best.

After Walker's fifth time through the course, McKellen blew the whistle and waved him over. "Bring it in, forty-six."

Panting, Walker came to a hard stop in front of the trainer, eager for the news. "What are we looking at?"

"Not too bad." McKellen's tone was neutral as he glanced up from his stopwatch, but the look in his eyes said it all.

Walker's gut clenched.

Doug "Mac" McKellen was a decent guy, helped train and rehab hockey players all over the country, NHL and college alike. Head Coach Gallagher had brought him in from Saint Paul to work with some of the injured guys on the team, but mostly for Walker, hoping they could get him back on the ice before the season ended. The dude was smart and straightforward, didn't pull any punches. So Walker knew before the man uttered another word that his damn times—while better than they'd been two months ago—still weren't strong enough to get him back into the starting lineup.

"Tell me what I need to do," Walker said.

"You need to tighten up your turns. Shave another twenty, thirty seconds off these times, minimum." McKellen glanced at the cones and shook his head. "And you need to do it again and again, bang on, every day, every time."

"Thirty seconds?" Swallowing his despair, Walker nodded brusquely. "Alright, Mac. Line 'em up. Let's go again."

Coach Gallagher, who'd been sitting quiet as a statue on the players' bench until now, folded his arms over his chest and shook his head. "Your edges are a mess, Dunn," he called out. "Turns are loose. Leg is dragging. You're hurtin' today, boy."

Yeah? You get your ass crushed in a rollover wreck, see how great your legs work.

Walker pinched the bridge of his nose, forcing himself to shake the foul attitude. The medics who'd dragged him out of that wreck said he was damn lucky to be alive, and most days, he believed them. But *damn*, the crash happened in June, and it was already the end of November. After six months of suffering nearly unbearable pain—and almost losing the ability to play entirely—he was truly starting to resent his own body.

"He's right, Walker," McKellen said, keeping his voice low, just between them. "I can see the pain in your face clear across the rink."

If there was one thing Walker hated more than being injured, it was people feeling sorry for him for being injured. And right now, McKellen's eyes were full of sympathy, voice thick as cough syrup. He'd take the coach's hard edges over that weepy bullshit any day.

"No pain, no gain, right?" he said, forcing a tight smile.

"Don't give me that bullshit," McKellen said. "Look, you keep pushing it out here, you'll put your entire recovery at risk. One fuck-up, and you're looking at riding the bench the rest of your life—not just on the hockey rink. That what you want?"

Walker jerked the helmet from his head, ran a hand through his sweat-drenched hair. He was losing steam, the adrenaline from his earlier successes draining out of him. "You know it isn't."

"Then you need to listen to me. To the docs. I know you're anxious to get back out there, but you need to let this recovery run its course. Your body will tell you when it's ready."

"Don't bullshit me, Mac. I don't have the luxury of letting this shit heal on its own timeline." Walker jerked his head toward the coach, keeping his voice in check, but just barely. "Term's almost up. If I don't get back on the active roster this season, they won't renew my contract, and then I'm out on my ass. Permanently."

Walker knew it, sure as he knew how to hold a stick and pass a puck. No matter how good he'd been in his prime, no matter how many records he'd broken, no matter how loyal he'd been to the Tempest, no NHL team would sign a washed-up puck jockey with a bum knee and shit times.

Walker tugged his helmet back into place. He *had* to make this work.

McKellen shook his head, blew out a frustrated breath. Holding up his hands in surrender, he said, "It's your life, son. Make the call."

"One more run, then we'll see where we're at." Without waiting for a response, Walker skated to the goal line at the other end of the rink as fast as he could, pivoting in a sharp turn in front of the net.

Bad idea.

He'd twisted too hard, thrown off his balance. His left foot slid ahead while his right knee stayed behind, and then he was on his ass, helmet skittering across the ice.

Another bolt of pain shot through his leg, radiating all the way up to his hip. He pulled himself up again, but it was a fight to stay on his feet, not to just crumple back to the ice like a fucking baby. Not to shut his eyes and let the darkness seep in.

Walker tried to tell himself it was just an off day. Not enough sleep last night, maybe, or hitting the free weights too hard at the gym this morning before the session. But the little nagging bitch who'd set up camp inside his head said otherwise, and as much as he'd tried to ignore that bitch, he couldn't ignore the searing pain.

His knee was on fire, and just like that, he was back in that car.

Swerving to miss the kid on the bike who'd darted out into the intersection, not even looking.

The screech of brakes, the smell of burnt rubber.

Metal on metal.

Broken glass.

Blood in his mouth.

Sirens.

Lucky to be alive...

"Walker." McKellen's hand clamped down over his shoulder, yanking Walker back to the present. "You good?"

Walker clenched his teeth, then opened his mouth and spit on the ice. There wasn't any blood—not really. His legs were straight. He was here, on the rink, in full pads, still fucking alive. He nodded.

"We're going to plan B," McKellen said, signaling to Coach.

Walker had no idea what the hell was going on, but he could already tell he wasn't going to like it. "What's plan B?"

McKellen looked at him a good long while, assessing. Whatever the man was looking for, Walker was pretty damn sure he didn't find it. Which sucked, because it was McKellen's recommendation that would get him back into the lineup, and the way the man was looking at Walker now… *fuck.*

Walker was bracing himself for the bad news when McKellen finally spoke. "Take five," he said. "Do a few easy laps. I need to talk to Gallagher."

Walker did a lap around the rink, his strides long and deliberate, slowly working the pain out of his joints. But the tension in his muscles remained, winding his insides tight as a drum.

There on the bench, it wasn't just McKellen and Gallagher anymore. The GM was there, too, along with the assistant coach, the team's lead doctor, and some stiff in a suit. The six of them sat together, heads bent over a clipboard, shrugging and nodding, his fate in their hands.

Walker sighed. He knew they were just looking out for him. Protecting their asset. Hell, they wanted him back on the ice almost as badly as he wanted it; before the wreck, he'd led the league in assists three years running. With his left and right wingers—Rob "Roscoe" LeGrand and Kyle "Henny" Henderson, two guys he'd take a fist, a body-check, *or* a bullet for—he'd helped make the Tempest the top-scoring team in the NHL last year. The rookie playing first line center now was better than some of the second- and third-line guys who'd been on the team for years—a damn good hockey player. But he wasn't *Walker Dunn* good.

Everyone on that bench knew it. His teammates knew it. Hell, everyone in the whole league knew it.

But they also knew Walker couldn't play with an injured knee. And after three separate surgeries, a fuck-load of physical therapy, pain meds up the ass, and endless workouts at the gym and on the ice, he'd hit a damn wall.

His times had plateaued. The pain was coming more frequently, lasting longer, requiring more pills to ease the ache each time. The docs had warned Walker about the possibility of a setback like this, but he'd shrugged it off. Accident aside, he was a world-class athlete at the top of his game, in better physical condition that most guys half his age.

He just wished his knee had gotten the fucking memo. Lately he'd been feeling more like a retiree than an athlete, and it showed. He could tell by the way management looked at him, a rage-inducing mix of frustration and pity, like they were ten seconds away from signing his death warrant. The guys sitting on the bench had the power to decide his future, and if Walker didn't get back in the game soon, retirement could be closer than he wanted to admit.

No, thirty-two years old wasn't exactly ancient in the NHL. But for every thirty- and forty-something career standout, there were a dozen twenty-year-old kids waiting in the wings, just as wild and hungry as

Walker had been at that age. And healthier. Stronger. Faster.

Hockey was Walker's thing. His *only* thing. He didn't know how to do anything else, how to be anyone else. Without the ice, without the uniform, without number forty-six, Walker was a damn ghost in his own life.

And no matter how bad it hurt, no matter how hard he had to push himself, Walker would not walk away from his career.

Not to mention the money.

Walker sighed, shook his head to clear his thoughts. It wasn't just about money—of course not. But anyone who said money couldn't solve problems? Hell, that guy must've had a better childhood than Walker.

That guy also didn't have a mother in a top-of-the-line Alzheimer's facility, or two younger brothers still in college. Dear old Dad had checked himself out of their lives years earlier, and if the docs were right about Mom —and when it came to the docs at Wellshire Place, they usually *were* right—it wouldn't be long before she couldn't recognize any of them.

Walker was all they had. Yeah, he loved hockey. Loved being on the ice. But he also loved taking care of his family. Looking out for them. Making sure they'd never know the pain and fear he'd felt as a kid, afraid to dream, afraid to think there might be a better life waiting out there. And while there was all kinds of suffering money *couldn't* help, Walker would die before he let his mother spend a night hungry, or cold, or reliving any of the myriad shitty things his father had put her through over the years. All of that was behind her now. Behind all of them.

And Walker had every intention of keeping it that way.

"Alright, forty-six. Here's the deal." McKellen skated over from the bench. Behind him, most of the others packed up and took off, leaving only Coach Gallagher. "We're trying a different approach. Got someone for you to meet."

How was that even possible? Walker felt like he'd already met with every coach, manager, doctor, physical therapist, and shrink in New York State. The only thing they hadn't subjected him to was hanging out with fans —an idea Gallagher had floated early on as a way to help him get his spirits up. Walker had immediately shot it down.

Good God, he hoped they weren't going there again.

"Please tell me it's not another groupie." Not that he didn't appreciate their enthusiasm, but as far as he was concerned, his job was to play hockey. Help his team get into the playoffs. And yeah, maybe entertaining the crowds during the games and at fundraisers was part of the gig, but that didn't mean he had to open up a vein and let them into his personal pain.

"Just someone who might be able to help. Assuming you're up for the challenge." McKellen pulled off his knit cap, raked a hand through his gray hair. He wouldn't meet Walker's eyes. "I'll be real honest with you, kid. You might not like it. But at this point, you don't have a choice."

The fuck?

"Just do us all a favor." McKellen finally looked at Walker, the warning clear in his eyes. "Don't scare her off."

CHAPTER TWO

There was a time in Eva Bradshaw's life—not that long ago, actually—when she had standards. When certain lines were more easily left uncrossed. When there were still a few things—okay, *one* thing—she swore she'd never, ever do.

Not even for money.

Avoiding her own gaze in the locker room mirror, she unhooked her plain beige bra, let it fall soundlessly to the bench.

Desperation had a funny way of eradicating a woman's principles.

"There has to be another way." Marybeth, Eva's sister, handed over a tight-fitting tank, shaking her head at Eva in the mirror. The concern was clear in her eyes, made all the more stark by the Hollywood-style light bulbs surrounding the glass. This wasn't the kind of chipped-tile, dented-lockers, bleach-and-sweat-scented dressing room Eva was used to. The benches here were mahogany, the lockers gleaming with fresh paint, every inch of the place decorated to make you feel like you actually deserved to be here.

Eva rolled her eyes. She'd been lucky to even get the invitation. "There isn't, Marybeth."

"But Mom—"

"Won't ever find out about this." Eva yanked the top down over her head and turned to face her sister, narrowing her eyes. She knew exactly what Marybeth was thinking, and yes, their mother would love nothing more than to swoop in with her third ex-husband's checkbook and save the day. But Eva couldn't—*wouldn't* —give her mother the satisfaction of asking for a loan. Not when Eva still had options—no matter how despicable those options might be. "I mean it, Marybeth. I'm trusting you here."

Marybeth sighed, crossing her arms over her chest. "I'm not telling Mom your dirty little secrets. I'm just worried about you."

"I've got this."

"That's what you said about—"

"Marybeth, honestly. It's just two hours with a man." A cocky, arrogant, dick-swinging man who could probably buy his way into and out of any possible situation, including the one she was about to get tangled up in right now.

Eva was more than familiar with the type; seven years ago, when she was still too young and idealistic to know better, she'd gotten up-close-and-personal with that particular brand of douche bag. The experience had left her broken, destroyed. And no matter how many years had passed, there would be no forgetting it—even if she'd wanted to.

But Eva had learned a lot from her past mistakes, and now she knew *exactly* how to handle guys like this. They were all the same—serious mommy issues. And like the man-babies they were, they needed boundaries. Clear expectations. Rules.

And if Walker Dunn didn't agree to the terms, she'd return his trainer's cash and call off the deal without a second thought. That simple.

Well, other than the part where she *really* needed that money.

Eva blew out a breath, then forced a smile she hoped looked reassuring. "Come on. How bad can it be?"

Marybeth raised an eyebrow. "I think we *both* know the answer to that question."

"Good. Then there's no need to rehash the past."

"Are you sure about that?"

No. "Yes," Eva said, sliding her plain cotton panties

down over her hips—they'd only get in the way. She folded
them into a triangle and set them on the bench next to her
jeans and beige bra, then quickly pulled on a pair of padded
spandex. She hoped this affair wouldn't be too hard on her
butt, but it was always better to be prepared, just in case.

"God, Eva. When did you turn into Mom?" Marybeth
wrinkled her nose at the boring undergarments on the
bench which—okay, fine—looked like a pile of old paper
bags. "I hope you don't wear that stuff on dates."

"What dates?" Eva turned back toward the mirror to
wrap her long hair into a bun, securing the loose strands
with bobby pins. "Anyway, I can't have nice things. Bilbo
Baggins chews through everything."

"Changing the subject to your oaf of a dog is not
going to work."

"He's not an oaf. He's just a little needy." Which was
fine by Eva. Unlike the two-legged men in her life, the
Saint Bernard had never disappointed her. Chewing
through her shoes, her purse, her underwear? Whatever.
She'd take that over getting her heart shredded any day.

"Eva. When was the last time you went out with a
man?" Marybeth rested her hands on her hips, her eyes
still full of concern that wasn't altogether misplaced—
just ill-timed. Marybeth was in a ridiculously happy
marriage with a man who'd given her the world, and she
truly believed that everyone deserved the kind of relationship that stole your breath away. And, like many

people who'd found their one-and-only, Marybeth honestly believed that epic, soul-shining love was out there, even for Eva, just waiting to be discovered.

Eva wasn't opposed to the idea. She hadn't sworn off *all* men—just hockey players. But even if what Marybeth believed was actually true—that she could find her soul mate if only she'd put in a little effort—Eva didn't have the time or the energy for a hunt like that. In her experience, men were unreliable at best, cruel and deceptive at worst, and she had other priorities right now.

The same priorities that had led her to this way-too-fancy locker room in the first place.

So why should she put her heart on the line? No way. Eva would rather rely on herself, no matter what challenges she faced.

"Well?" Marybeth asked, handing Eva her pink fleece.

"Hmm… the last time I went out with a man…" Eva cocked her head and tapped her chin, pretending to consider the question. "Does today count?"

"Pro-tip, sis. It's not a date when they're paying you."

"Oh, right. I must've skipped that part of the handbook." Eva zipped up her fleece and gathered her regular clothes, tucking them into the oversized locker where she'd already stashed her snow boots and overcoat. Turning back to her sister with another forced smile, she said, "Thank you for your concern, Marybeth, and for your undying devotion to my love life. But—"

"*Lack* of love life."

Eva shrugged. "I have you and Nate. And I have Gracie."

Gracie, Eva's six-year-old daughter, was the reason she got out of bed in the morning. The reason she was here right now, sweating in her padded spandex and fleece, already counting the money Walker's trainer had promised her.

"Not to mention Bilbo Baggins," Marybeth dead-panned. "Who eats your underwear."

"A small price to pay for his endless affection."

After a beat, Marybeth sighed and said, "Are you all set, then? Do you need me to pick up Gracie after school?"

"Don't you have students today?" Eva asked. Marybeth was a reading specialist who worked one-on-one out of her home office with kids who needed more individualized attention. She set her own schedule, like Eva, which meant that the sisters could be there for each other at a moment's notice.

Eva had always appreciated that, especially when it came to Gracie, who adored her Aunt Marybeth and Uncle Nate. But at the same time, accepting help—even from family—had always been challenging for Eva. Marybeth truly had a heart of gold, but their mother operated from an entirely different place. Sure, she'd do anything for anyone, but not until she'd let the whole world know about the great sacrifices she'd made for you, lording it over you for all eternity.

It was bad enough the woman was covering Gracie's school tuition, reminding Eva about her own failures as a mother at every turn.

Last year, after Eva discovered that Gracie had endured months of emotional torment by a group of boys twice her size—bullies which the school adminis-tration refused to expel on account of their parents being so-called "prominent" members of the community —Eva yanked her right out of that school and enrolled her in a private elementary school. The change in her daughter had been almost instantaneous—Gracie thrived, making new friends and excelling in her class, her familiar smile even brighter than before. But Eva's salary wasn't enough to cover the tuition and costs over the long haul.

Enter her mother, who'd swept in and pre-paid the tuition for the entire school year, and who was already telling her neighbors that she'd be "sacrificing her own retirement plans in order to fund her granddaughter's education, probably through college."

Normally, Eva wouldn't take her mother's charity— their relationship was perilous enough without adding money into the mix. But when it came to Gracie, Eva swallowed her pride. It was no match for her daughter's well-being. For her happiness.

Still, it wasn't a permanent solution. Eva would not stand by and let her daughter become another victim of Grandma's martyrdom, especially as the girl got older. Eva knew firsthand that once Gracie hit a certain age, Grandma's so-called kindness would transform into something dark and cruel, a weight around Gracie's neck, just as it had been around Eva's for her entire life.

Yes, it was a screwed-up dynamic—one Eva was pretty certain would keep a therapist busy for decades, if she ever decided to see somebody. But for now, Eva needed to find a way to pay her mother back, to cut her out of the family finances. To truly take care of Gracie. To plan for their future.

"My afternoon appointment canceled," Marybeth said now. "Poor kid has mono. So I'm around if you need me."

Eva dug the phone out from the bottom of her purse and glanced at the screen, which was currently covered in *Star Wars* stickers and something that smelled suspiciously like grape jelly. Eva smiled. Gracie's handiwork was just another reminder of why she was here today.

She scraped off the stickers with her thumbnail and checked the time, ignoring the icky residue. "Assuming this guy isn't a total freak show, I should be out of here in time."

"Okay. Let me know if anything changes." Marybeth tried to sound casual, but Eva picked up on the concern lingering in her sister's voice.

"Promise," Eva said, grabbing her duffel bag and slinging it over her shoulder like the pro that she was. She'd finish gearing up once she got out there.

Marybeth shut the locker door. "Anything at all."

"Yep," Eva said, but nothing was going to change. Eva had accepted the trainer's ridiculously generous offer over the phone—a two-hour session, $500 in cash— because she needed that money, the sooner the better, and this was the least complicated way to get it.

No matter that the thought of what waited on the other side of that door filled her with dread.

No matter that she was trying to raise a strong, inde- pendent daughter who'd never be reduced to a bundle of anxious nerves at the thought of dealing with a man like Walker Dunn.

And no matter that once upon a time, seven years ago, she'd made a solemn promise to never, *ever* get hot and sweaty with a hockey player again.

CHAPTER THREE

"*She's* your grand plan?" Walker folded his arms over his chest as a woman skated out onto the ice, her strides long and graceful, like something out of a little girl's music box.

Yep. A woman. On skates. Dressed in a fitted pink fleece and a pair of black spandex pants that hugged every curve, her red hair wrapped up in a prissy little bun right on top of her head.

Walker laughed, wondering whether the rest of the guys had anything to do with this unexpected little present, or if it was just the bosses. Normally he'd be all over it, but at the moment, he was a long way from normal. It was hard enough keeping a clear head with his knee throbbing like a motherfucker. Walker didn't need to get anything else throbbing today.

"Her name's Evangeline Bradshaw," McKellen said.

"And she's not cheap, so I suggest you make the most of your time together."

"How much time we talking?"

"You've got her for two hours today. We'll see how it goes after that."

Walker shook his head. Did they really think he was that desperate? He'd only been riding the bench a handful of months—on the ice and in the bedroom. He'd had no say in the former, but the latter was his choice; since the accident, he'd brought only one woman home —someone he'd met at a bar last month. They hadn't even taken their clothes off. Walker had called a car for her after one round of drinks, feigning a migraine. He just couldn't get into it. Not that night, and not any night since.

But *getting* the women wasn't the problem—never had been—and he certainly didn't need help in that department from his coaches. His bosses. And he absolutely did *not* need anyone paying for it.

Hell, wasn't there a law against that kind of shit?

He took another look at Evangeline, wondering what the fuck her story was. Long, lean legs. That uptight little bun. Fuzzy pink fleece. Probably liked a man to hold her close, whisper in her ear, all that chocolate-and-roses bullshit. Definitely not the kind to want her hair pulled, to let him take her hard and fast against the wall as she screamed his name, over and over...

"You hear me, Dunn?"

Walker shook his head again and laughed, clapping McKellen hard on the back. "No offense, Mac, but you don't even know my type."

"Far as I'm concerned, your type is anyone who can deal with your bullshit long enough to get you back in the game."

Walker watched as the woman glided toward them, her long legs graceful and powerful as they stroked across the ice.

She *was* gorgeous—no denying that, even from halfway across the rink. Flame red hair Walker imagined spilling down her back. Taut little body that was probably flexible enough to do just about anything his dirty mind could imagine. And hell, that woman had *presence*. He could feel it radiating off her from the moment she'd stepped onto the ice.

"Whose idea was this?" he asked, not taking his eyes off her.

"Mine. It's not unheard of, Walker. I've made arrangements like this for a few players over the years— guys who needed a different approach. A boost to help them get back on track."

Walker's mouth curled up at the corner. Apparently, Mac had a kinky side that Walker had yet to fully appreciate. Alright, maybe he'd dismissed the idea too quickly. It'd been a while since that epic fail with the woman from the bar. Maybe a long, slow night with the too-sweet good girl was *exactly* what he needed to help him unwind, burn off some of his pent-up energy. Even if she *was* uptight, Walker was pretty sure he could teach her a thing or two between the sheets, help her unleash her hidden wildcat. Make it a good night for *both* of them.

His dick stirred at the thought. If not for his protective gear, everyone on the rink would've gotten an eyeful —including the woman, who'd finally glided to a stop in front of them.

She was keeping her face neutral, not quite meeting his gaze, but behind the cold-as-ice exterior, she couldn't hide those soft, soulful brown eyes. Lush, kissable lips. That red hair. She was... *damn*. Walker didn't even have the words for it. He'd been around beautiful women before—gorgeous women, state after state, country after country, each one a fond memory to heat up his lonely winter nights. But there was something about this woman that completely captivated him. That presence, he thought. She hadn't even made eye contact yet, but he could fucking *feel* it, like the crackle in the air before a lightning storm.

"This is Evangeline Bradshaw," McKellen said. "She'll be working with you for the rest of the afternoon, providing you can act like a gentleman."

"Working?" *Interesting choice of words.* Walker choked back a laugh, but McKellen didn't look amused.

SYLVIA PIERCE

In fact, he looked dead serious.

"She's a two-time Olympic medalist," McKellen went on. "Renowned skating coach. And possibly your only shot at getting your speed and balance back."

Jesus fucking Christ.

Walker's dick shrunk, right along with his hopes.

No, they hadn't found him a woman to spend a few hot, steamy hours with. They'd hired an ice princess to teach him how to skate.

As if he hadn't grown up on the ice.

As if he'd lost all those years of hard lessons, hard work, hard-won experience right along with his mobility.

As if they could just make these decisions for him. About him.

A figure skater.

Teaching *him* how to play hockey.

Walker glared at McKellen. "Yeah, well. As much as I'd love to practice my twirls and jumps, I'm late for my ballet class. And after that, I'm having a facial, maybe a mani-pedi." He wriggled his fingers in jest, but anger and frustration slithered along his spine, twin snakes ready to bite. He didn't care about taking one for the team now, about proving his commitment to recovery. He'd done everything in his power to show them how much he wanted back in, and *this* was their answer? Their grand plan to get him back in shape?

26

Fuck this.

Captivating woman or not, Walker wasn't about to accept this. He turned his back on them both. "I'm outta here."

"Actually, you're not." Evangeline what's-her-name finally spoke up, her tone firm and commanding. Walker was so surprised, he stopped in his tracks, turning around to face her.

She skated right up to him, toe-to-toe. Her eyes, he saw now, weren't brown. They were the color of honey, amber, shot through with yellow and gold and other colors he couldn't even name. They flashed at him from beneath thick lashes, her cheeks blushing.

"And you're going to stop me?" he asked.

Those amber eyes blazed, pinning him to his spot on the ice. "Believe it or not, Mr. Dunn, I've got better things to do today than babysit your ego."

"*Excuse* me, princess?"

Jerking her head toward McKellen, she said, "Your trainer and coach stressed to me the importance of your recovery—how hard you were willing to work. Said you'd do *anything* to get off the bench. Did they mislead me?"

Walker felt the weight of McKellen's stare heating his skin. There was only one right answer here, unless he wanted to walk away from all of it right now—for good.

"No," he said, finally checking his ego. The anger drained out of him fast.

God, he'd been a total dickbag, taking out his frustration on this woman. Assuming she was there for his pleasure, then huffing and puffing like an ornery kid when he found out she wasn't.

When did he become such a low-class asshole?

"So I'm *not* keeping you from ballet?" she asked.

"No, ma'am." He offered what he hoped was an apologetic smile, but she wasn't having it.

"Then I suggest you drop the attitude so we can get to work. Your coaches aren't paying me to stand around and look pretty, and I doubt that's what *you're* getting paid for, either."

"I..." He clamped his mouth shut. *Did she just call me pretty?*

Her tone would've made him bristle—*should* have made him bristle—but he was too damn intrigued to admit just how much she pissed him off. It was a dangerous combination, but at this point, what the fuck did he have to lose?

Besides, for some supremely fucked-up reason he couldn't even *begin* to guess at, he wanted to prove himself to her. He wanted her to know he was serious, professional. Talented. Not a dickbag.

"Are we all on the same page now?" McKellen asked, shooting another warning glare at Walker.

"We're good," Walker said.

After what felt like an eternity, McKellen nodded, then skated back to the bench to talk with the coach.

Walker shook his head, clearing his thoughts. He couldn't afford to piss them off. He needed to get his shit together—physically *and* mentally.

"Olympics, huh?" He turned to face Evangeline, struck again by those fiery amber eyes. "That's pretty fucking badass, Evangeline."

"Eva," she said. "And you bet your ass it is." Her tone had thawed a fraction, the ghost of a smile playing on her lips.

Walker returned it with a cocky grin of his own. Neither of them looked away, the silence building between them like a dare.

"So. You ready?" She arched a perfectly shaped brow —a challenge he was finally ready to accept.

"Think you can teach this old dog a few new tricks?"

"Depends," she said coolly. Without warning, she shot backward, skates swizzling against the ice, propelling her lithe body across the rink and leaving his ass in the dust as she taunted him one last time. "Think you can keep up, old dog?"

CHAPTER FOUR

Despite the icy air and the nerves in her belly, Eva's blood was on fire.

Infuriating. Cocky. Unappreciative. Entitled. Capital-R Rude.

In the span of five minutes, Walker Dunn had earned every one of those qualifiers ten times over. But holy hell, what the man lacked in manners, he more than made up for in other ways.

Ways that pushed Eva's sex-starved imagination into overdrive, her thighs clenching beneath the spandex even as she rocketed herself backward, far away from his intimidating presence.

Eva prided herself on her professionalism. On her ability to remain cool and detached in the face of even the most demanding clients. And on a personal level, while she considered herself fairly open-minded when it came to sex, hockey boys were what she liked to call her hard limit.

No way. No how. Never again.

Despite the ample opportunity her on-ice career had afforded her, she'd kept that vow for years. But from the moment she'd seen Walker up close, all swagger and snarl, something inside her cracked loose, exposing a soft spot that was supposed to have stayed walled up for eternity.

She'd beat him to the edge of the rink, and now he skated toward her, hard and powerful, his steel-gray eyes locked on hers like a weapon. God, it had been way too long since she'd been with a man, and her mind wandered into a dangerous fantasyland, serving up red-hot images of Walker pinning her against the boards, his mouth claiming hers in a vicious kiss. She wondered what he smelled like up close, in the warm curve where his neck met his shoulder. She wondered what his mouth tasted like, how his two-day stubble would feel scratching against her face. Her neck. Her thighs. She wondered what it might feel like to slide underneath him, pinned down by those powerful, muscular arms as he growled hot and low in her ear.

The thought nearly undid her.

Never again, never again, never again…

Eva repeated the mantra until she got it under control, reminding herself that all that fantasizing was just the animal part of her brain, reacting to the stimulus of his raw, masculine sex appeal. The *rational* part of her brain knew damn well that Walker Dunn was just another hockey boy looking to score, and right now, that rational brain needed just one thing:

To kick his egotistical ass all the way back down the rink. Show him who was boss, establish those boundaries she kept talking about, and squash that sex-starved little cavewoman inside her before she got herself into a situation she couldn't get out of.

Walker finally approached, and Eva shot him an icy glare. "Nice of you to show up," she said. "I thought maybe you'd decided to call a cab."

He skated right up close, pointed a finger at her chest. "*You* don't play fair, princess."

His tone was laced with annoyance, but there was a playful spark in his eyes that did something to her insides.

Steeling herself against his obvious charms, Eva skated a backward circle around him, forcing him to turn to keep his eyes on her. "Do the guys on the other teams play fair?" she asked. "Do they print out a list of all their moves ahead of time, let you peek at the playbook so you know exactly what to expect?"

When he didn't respond, she continued. "You need to be ready for anything, forty-six. So if you can't read their minds, read their body language. And then—"

"Hey, thanks for the 101, but I'm pretty sure I remember how to play hockey."

"*And then,*" she continued, refusing to be interrupted, "make sure you're faster than them. Always."

"I *am* fast."

Eva stopped moving long enough to catch his gaze and hold it. "So why am I here?"

"You're here because my coach and trainer like screwing with me. I don't need lessons on how to play."

Eva considered his words, and more importantly, all the things he *wasn't* saying. His trainer had told her how he'd been riding the bench since his accident, unable to fully recover, even with the team's best doctors, state-of-the-art equipment, and intensive personal training. She understood that it had to be hard for him, knowing he might never play again. Might never have a chance to follow his passion. On some level, she could relate to that.

But he was also acting like a spoiled child. Didn't really surprise her, but it *was* starting to piss her off.

Time to make her point, fast and hard.

"You're right," she said evenly. "You don't need lessons on how to play. But you *do* need to get those drill times back up. I can help with that, if you let me."

He crossed his bulky arms over his chest and glared at her. "How?"

"It's all a matter of physics." She thumbed toward the

other end of the ice. "Show me what you've got, forty-six."

"You mean you don't already know? I thought you were the expert here."

"I need to see what I'm dealing with so I can determine the best course of action."

"But you—"

"Chop chop, forty-six. There and back, as fast as you can. On my mark, okay?"

With a great, overdramatic sigh, Walker finally relented. He crouched into position, ready to launch himself across the rink.

His body was rigid, his jaw clenched, all six-feet-five-inches of him poised to attack that distance, chew it up like his life depended on it. Eva could see a half-dozen mistakes in his stance alone—the way he leaned forward, banking on confidence and strength over agility and efficiency.

"You ready?" she asked, finger hovering over the stopwatch button.

"Are *you*?" Wasting no more time, Walker took off down the ice.

He didn't glide so much as stomp, his strides strong but lumbering. There was no doubt he was a powerhouse—despite his bulk, the weight of the gear, and his injury, Walker was still pretty damn fast on those blades. But he was straining, pushing hard to prove a point. If he exerted this much energy during an actual game, he wouldn't last five minutes.

Walker banked at the end of the rink and boomeranged around the net, charging toward her once again. Keeping her eyes locked on his legs, Eva catalogued his movements, noticed where his right leg dragged, how hard he favored the bad knee. It threw off his balance, messed with his momentum, and severely limited his ability to do what needed to be done.

Worse, he was in pain—a lot more than he was admitting. One look at his clenched jaw and furrowed brow told her that.

A pinprick of guilt poked her chest, but she dismissed it. Walker Dunn was a grown man who should know his own limitations. If he was serious about getting back into the game, he needed to be honest about those limitations so they could work through them together.

Eva stopped the timer.

Walker threw a cocky grin her way as he slid to a stop, spraying her skates with ice. The attitude was authentic, but the grin was forced; angry blotches of red covered his face, his chest heaving with the effort.

But damn, those smoky gray eyes wouldn't let her off the hook for anything. They sparkled beneath his dark, sweat-drenched hair, flashing with challenge.

"Fast enough for you?" he asked.

"Not bad," she said, trying to dodge his penetrating

gaze... and then trying not to think about the word *penetrating* while standing so close to him.

Is it hot in here? I think it's hot in here...

Eva unzipped the top half of her fleece.

"Not *bad*?" He leaned forward and raised a brow that would've set her panties on fire, had she been wearing any. A drop of sweat fell from his hair and slid down his cheek, tracing a path through the stubble along his jaw. In a low growl, he said, "I suppose you could do better, princess?"

Eva backed away, putting some much-needed space between them. "I'm not the one trying to get back on the roster."

"In other words, you're all talk."

He was baiting her. She knew it, felt that hook sliding into her like a caught fish.

Yet she took it. Every inch of it.

Dammit.

Before Eva's beloved father passed away several years ago, he'd always said that she'd inherited her competitive nature from him; that it was the best part of her. Her unwillingness to back down from a challenge had made her a force on the U.S. Olympics Team, earning medals and sponsorships, helping her achieve nearly impossible dreams. But her mother had always said it'd made her obstinate and stubborn, impossible to deal with, and—on Mom's particularly smug days—unlikely to ever find a man.

They were both a little bit right, and in the years since she'd left the competition, Eva had done her level best to keep her ego in check, showing her coaching clients just enough of her skills to understand that they'd be getting their money's worth from her, but never pushing it. Never making them feel small just to prove how damn good she really was.

But all of that carefully honed self-restraint flew right out the window when Walker Dunn smirked at her.

"I wanna see your so-called physics in action," he said. "Otherwise I'm not buying your story. And if I'm not buying it, you can bet your ass McKellen isn't buying it."

Eva tried not to roll her eyes. McKellen *was* buying it —they'd already agreed on payment, regardless of how the session turned out today. But that didn't mean Eva could let Walker get away with this.

Something inside her clicked and sparked, an old feeling she hadn't realized how much she'd missed. Eva hadn't skated competitively in years, but the fire was there again in an instant, as if it had never left. The heat started deep in her belly, quickly spreading outward into her limbs until she was nearly engulfed, consumed by the need to prove herself. To shut him up, shut him down, and wipe that infuriating smile off his way-too-handsome-to-be-legal face.

"You need a demonstration, forty-six? You got it." She skated backward toward the other end of the rink. "I'll start down at the goal line. You start here. When you see me take off from that spot, you come at me. Hard and fast as you can."

"And then?" He was still flashing that infuriating smile.

"Try to catch me. Knock me on my ass."

"That all?" Walker laughed, shaking his head. "Sorry, princess. Not happening."

"Of course it isn't. You won't even get close." Eva didn't wait for another response—she was already speeding down to the goal line. She stopped in front of the net and turned to face him, her body warm, blood buzzing with adrenaline.

Let's do this…

She pushed off from her toe pick and rocketed down the ice, Walker coming straight at her, picking up more speed, more power with every stroke. The icy air whipped her cheeks, making her eyes water, turning her surroundings into a blur. If the two stayed on their current course, they'd collide in t-minus five, four, three…

Walker was holding back, just like she knew he would.

Even as he zoomed toward her, he held out his arms, already preparing to cushion her fall. She let him think he was about to do just that. Then, in the span of a heartbeat, Eva shifted her weight away from him, bending like a ribbon in the wind, no bones, no lines, just pure energy.

Tension crackled in the air as two powerful bodies whooshed past each other, skates cutting across the ice. Eva picked up speed, pumping her legs as she skated hard for the goal line, then whipped back around to face Walker for round two.

He was a beast, grinding harder now, no more holding back. McKellen and Gallagher whooped from the bench, egging Walker on.

Again, Eva waited until she and Walker were nearly on top of each other, then twisted away just as Walker grabbed at empty air between them. They bounced back around their opposite nets for another go, and although Walker was really pushing himself, he missed her yet again. After the fourth go-round, Eva waved her hands to signal the game was over.

Walker bent over on the ice, hands on his knees, trying to catch his breath. He was still panting when Eva skated over to him, cutting her blades at the last second, spraying him with ice.

Ha! You should see my triple/triple!

Walker raised his eyes, glaring at her from beneath

his thick, black lashes. "Point..." he panted. "Point taken."

Eva fought to keep the smug smile from her face as Walker, for the first time since their meeting, was shocked into silence.

That playful spark in his eyes was gone now, shoved aside by anger and frustration. But looking past all that red-hot rage, Eva saw something else in his eyes: Respect.

And there, just beyond the respect, was the molten core of something else. Something that Eva felt, too. Something that—if left unchecked—would destroy her.

Walker Dunn was completely, unapologetically turned on.

CHAPTER FIVE

"Nice work, Miss Bradshaw." Doug McKellen held out a thick manila envelope. "Been a long time since anyone could wipe that smirk off his face."

Eva sat down on one of the benches behind the safety glass and returned his smile, pocketing the envelope without counting the cash inside. She could tell by its bulk that it was probably more than what they'd agreed on over the phone—more than she'd ever made in a one-on-one session.

"So what do you think?" McKellen asked. "What's our plan of attack here?"

Eva blew out a breath, trying to release some of the adrenaline that still coursed through her body. Out on the rink, Walker was talking with his head coach, nodding at something the coach was saying. They didn't seem to be arguing, but tension was rolling off Walker's body in waves.

All told, she and Walker had worked together for more than ninety minutes, zooming back and forth across the rink, running through extensive drills and exercises designed to push him to the limit of his capabilities and give her a more complete picture of the issues. To her surprise, after their initial confrontation, he'd done as she'd asked for the rest of the session without complaint. But she could tell his heart wasn't in it. Whether it was the pain in his knee or the blow to his ego, something was holding him back, putting up an invisible wall between them that would severely limit her ability to help him, no matter how much he was willing to push through the pain.

"Walker's a hockey player, through and through," Eva finally said, slipping her feet out of the ice skates. "He was trained to go after the puck, to knock down anyone in his way, to hustle for the net—that's it. No finesse. He skates like a gorilla on a rampage, and he's wasting a lot of energy doing it."

"That gorilla on a rampage leads the league in assists," McKellen said.

"That was before the injury," she said. "Frankly, lots of hockey players skate like that, and they get by just fine. But for Walker, it's different now. That knee is holding him back. Aside from total recovery, his best shot at getting back into the game is to become a more efficient skater, develop some techniques that would allow him to conserve energy while skating faster and smarter, and hopefully strengthening his knee in the process."

"So in your opinion, if we can teach him these techniques, there's a chance he'll improve?"

"A chance? Sure. I mean, I'm not a doctor. But I can tell you right now he'd shave some serious time off those drills."

"But...?" McKellen pinched the bridge of his nose and sighed. "I can hear it in your voice, Miss Bradshaw. Spit it out."

Eva hesitated, not sure how much more candid she should be. The man did just hand over a sizable lump of cash, and Eva didn't want to sound smug. She'd used up all that negative energy on the ice, and she'd intended to leave it there.

But he'd paid her to do a job, and she wasn't about to mislead him just for the sake of being nice.

"My honest assessment?" Eva fished through her gear bag for a soft cloth and began wiping down the blades of her skates. "Your man is all attitude, Mr. McKellen. I don't know if it's the injury or if he's always been like that, but it's holding him back."

McKellen offered a small smile. "Little of both, I'm afraid."

"It's more than that, too," she said. "Despite all that macho, smart-ass swagger, he's seriously hurting—and not just on the outside." She looked up at McKellen, who was watching her intently, considering her assessment. "Unless he can get that under control, all the training in the world won't help him."

McKellen nodded. She wasn't telling him anything he didn't know already.

"Sorry I don't have better news for you, Mr. McKellen. I'm just not sure what you thought we could fix in a couple of hours."

"I didn't bring you in for a quick fix." McKellen sat down next to her. "How would you feel about committing to a six-week program? A few mornings a week, help get our man back in the game?"

Eva blinked. Six weeks? With Walker Dunn? "I, um... I appreciate the vote of confidence, but I'm not a hockey expert, and—"

"Walker doesn't need a hockey expert. He needs a skating expert. Someone who can shake things up, break him out of his routine. Challenge him. Boost his confidence."

"And you think I'm the woman for the job?" she asked.

"Based on what I saw out there today? You bet." McKellen blew out a breath. "Look. We've been working with him for months. Coaches. Trainers. Even his teammates. None of us have been able to get through to him."

Blades clean and dry, Eva slid the skates back into her bag and looked out at Walker and his coach, their heads still bent together in conversation. Walker's shoulders slumped. She wondered what they were talking about, where Walker's head was at after the workout they'd endured. The man had put up so many walls, Eva couldn't even tell if he *wanted* to play hockey anymore.

"What makes you think *I* can get through to him?" she asked.

"You already did." McKellen nodded toward the rink. "This is the longest he's stayed out on the ice since the injury. I haven't been able to get him to do those slalom drills at all. Before you showed up, he was almost ready to call it a day. But he didn't. You worked his ass off out there, Miss Bradshaw. And he wanted to show you he could handle it. I don't know what you said to him, but he *was* listening—that much is clear."

The words sent a warm flush through her chest, the same feeling she got when any of her students finally nailed a difficult combo or got back up after a nasty fall. But the difference here was that Walker, unlike her students, didn't want her help. McKellen could say whatever he wanted; Eva had *felt* Walker's frustration with her. His disdain.

Not to mention his desire…

Eva tugged at the collar of her fleece, heat creeping up her neck. As if he could sense her thoughts, Walker looked up, catching her eyes from across the ice. Even at a distance, she could see the heat there, feel it as if it were a live wire. His gaze was locked on hers, unwavering and intense, and when he flashed her half a grin, her thighs clenched involuntarily.

There was her answer. No. There was simply no way she could say yes to six weeks on the ice with that man.

"Whatever your standard rate is for private coaching," McKellen said, "We'll double it. And if you're a morning person, you can have the ice for two hours before each session for your own use—rink's free at that time."

Despite her best efforts to be cool, Eva's eyes went wide with shock.

Never mind the ice time. Eighteen sessions, at double her rates? That was a *lot* of money. Enough to get them through the holidays and into the new year. Enough to start paying off her mother. Enough to get some new clothes for Gracie, whose pants and shirts were all wearing out at the knees and elbows, her ankles peeking out at the hems. Poor kid didn't even have a decent pair of snow boots—her little toes got soaked every time she stayed outside more than an hour. Eva had taken to lining her boots with plastic bags.

"That... that's a generous offer," she said, her earlier

reservations already melting away. She needed that money. The timing could not be better. Besides, if she planned it right, she could drop Gracie off at school instead of putting her on the bus, then hit the rink for some time on the ice before Walker showed up. She'd be done in plenty of time to pick Gracie up from school. And Marybeth always watched Gracie during the school's winter break—Marybeth had the same days off.

Plus, she could still meet with her other clients on the off days.

The whole thing was kind of perfect.

A smile stretched across her face.

"That a yes?" he asked.

Eva nodded. "Yes. Thank you."

"Can you start tomorrow? I don't want to wait too long to get Walker into the new routine."

"Tomorrow works," she said. "As long as it works for Walker."

"It will." McKellen held her gaze for a moment, then reached into his pocket for what looked like a business card. "Look, let me be real honest with you here. This isn't just about Walker. I run a training facility based in Minnesota. We're looking to bring in a top-notch figure skater to help us design and run immersive training camps for the NHL and some of the college teams."

Eva took the card, her head spinning.

"If you can get Walker up to snuff, and you're interested in something like this, I think we could make it happen."

"What are you saying, exactly?" she asked. She needed him to be absolutely clear.

"I'm saying I have an opening for a permanent position. Full time. Full benefits. Salary, healthcare, retirement, all of it. We have a state-of-the-art facility, really great people, too."

"In Minnesota," she said.

McKellen nodded. "Hey, at least you're already used to the snow. Right?"

Eva laughed. She'd grown up here in Buffalo. Used to the snow? She couldn't imagine winter without it.

"Relocation expenses would be covered, of course." McKellen stood up and lightly touched her shoulder. "Think about it, Miss Bradshaw. At the end of your time with Walker, if you decide the position isn't for you, well... no hard feelings. You're still walking away with a nice chunk of change for the holidays." Then, chuckling, "Hell, I bet Dunn would even sign a jersey for you, you play your cards right."

Lucky me.

Eva thanked him and promised her consideration, her mind already flipping through the possibilities as McKellen skated back out to Walker and the coach. She'd never had a regular, steady job before—something her mother was constantly throwing in her face.

This offer was an amazing opportunity with great perks and an even better paycheck. And Minnesota? That wasn't too far. An easy flight. Road trip distance, even.

No, it wasn't her dream of Olympic level competition, but those days were long over. This was an actual job that would allow her to use her passion for skating to help other people. The kind of job that meant a real shot at stability for her and Gracie—long-term stability. A future. A chance to get out from under her debts and her mother's crushing thumb.

A fresh start in a place she could make her own. Hers and Gracie's.

A warm, happy feeling spread through Eva's chest, a feeling full of hope and possibility where for so long she'd felt only worry and fear. As far as she could tell, the whole arrangement came with only one serious downside.

A 250-pound, impossibly gorgeous, infuriatingly rude downside who was suddenly skating right for her, that cocky, panty-melting grin waking up the parts of her body that were supposed to stay permanently asleep.

Walker slammed into the glass in front of her, still smirking. "Just heard the news. Looks like you and I are about to get *real* cozy."

Eva lifted her chin, trying to maintain her composure. "You'd better bring your A-game, forty-six. Today was just a prequel. Here on out, I'm going to work you so hard, you'll be crying for your mama."

"Mmm." Walker tapped his lips, his gaze drinking her in from top to bottom and back again, finally coming to rest on her mouth. The look in his eyes made her instantly wet. "*You* bring your A-game, princess. I like it rough."

CHAPTER SIX

Walker rolled out of bed the next morning feeling like he'd been shoved into a sack and tossed down a flight of stairs.

Twice.

Fuuuuck.

Trying to ignore the ache in his muscles, he dragged himself out of bed and into the kitchen to start the coffee. After his supreme ass-beating on the rink yesterday, he'd gone to Wellshire Place to visit his mom, then spent the rest of the night icing his knee and pouring shots of whiskey down his throat in a failed attempt to numb himself from head to toe.

All he'd gotten for his efforts was a pounding headache and a mouth full of cotton. And in less than an hour, he was due back at the rink for a fresh day of hell with his new coach. A pain in the ass new coach. A hot as fuck new coach who would look just about perfect in his bed, writhing underneath him, screaming his name in ecstasy, eyes rolled back in her head as Walker fucked her mindless.

But damn, that view was a far cry from the one he'd gotten yesterday, the ice princess kicking his ass up and down the rink, that smug little know-it-all smile plastered on her face.

It's all a matter of physics… chop-chop, forty-six…

Walker grabbed a bottle of aspirin from the counter and tossed a few back, ignoring the pulse of heat that throbbed in his cock, now straining against his sweatpants. He hated to admit it, but he kind of liked that Eva had called him by his number. Kind of wondered what it might sound like mixed in with a few other choice phrases…

Harder, forty-six. Right there, forty-six. That feels soooo good, forty-six…

"Dude. Seriously?" A harsh laugh yanked him out of the fantasy. "I mean, I know you're happy to see me, but…"

Roscoe, his left winger and best friend, stood in the back doorway off the kitchen, kicking snow off his boots and staring pointedly at Walker's crotch.

Walker turned his back on him and reached into the dishwasher for a clean mug. "Remind me why I don't have an alarm system?"

"You could start by locking your doors," Roscoe said. "Maybe getting a guard dog."

"Logan's allergic." His brothers were away at college, one in Ohio and one in Colorado, but they still technically lived with him. Logan's face would puff up like a blowfish at the first whiff of dog.

"That coffee fresh?" Roscoe asked.

"Yep." Walker grabbed the pot and filled up his mug. If Roscoe wanted some, he could get it his own damn self. "Close the door. I'm not paying to heat the whole outside."

"You are such a dad this morning. And by dad, I mean dickhead." Roscoe closed the door and kicked off his wet boots, laughing like a hyena. "So who's the lucky girl, Mr. McStiffy?"

"Nunya."

"Nunya?"

"Yeah, I think you've met her before. Nunya fuckin' business? Ring any bells?"

"Oh, so you're *not* thinking about fucking your new coach anymore?"

Walker grunted. He was a little fuzzy on the details, but he was pretty sure he'd already given Roscoe and Henny the rundown in a series of drunken texts last night. He was also pretty sure Roscoe had offered to tag along today, video the session to see if he could give Walker any pointers.

In the middle of his half-drunken stupor last night, it'd seemed like a decent idea. Now, he wasn't so sure.

"She's off-limits," Walker said. "Just so we're clear."

"Ahh." Roscoe pointed an accusatory finger at his chest. "So you *do* want her."

"I didn't say that. I just don't want you interfering with our professional relationship."

"You are professionally full of shit. Like, professionally."

"You're right." Walker tore open a banana, shoving half of it into his mouth in one bite. The more he thought about it, the more it chapped his ass. "Fuck it. I need to call McKellen, tell him I can't do it."

"Yeah, no. Not happening," Roscoe said. Before Walker could grab his phone from the counter, Roscoe swiped it and slid it into his back pocket. "Let it go, man."

"Seriously?"

"They're just looking out for you," Roscoe said. "For the team. All of us are."

Walker rolled his eyes. "Do me a favor, sunshine. Dial down the kumbaya until I get a little more caffeine in me." He jammed the rest of the banana into his mouth, then chucked the peel at Roscoe, hitting him square in the face.

"Dude." Without missing a beat, Roscoe winged it right back at him, but Walker dodged, and the peel hit the edge of the sink with a wet slap. It reminded him of horsing around with his brothers, and for a second he relaxed. Almost smiled.

"Look at the bright side," Roscoe said. "She might actually *help* your sorry ass."

Roscoe believed it, too. Real "bright side" kind of guy. Good for mid-game locker room pep talks. Shitty for days when all Walker wanted to do was punch something.

Walker *knew* the coaches were looking out for him— they wanted him back on the team, and the team needed him—but still. Why couldn't they man up and talk to him about this new plan ahead of time? About this figure skater? This infuriating, masochistic woman who'd gotten off on torturing him yesterday like it was some kind of sick game?

Walker bristled, his muscles aching at the reminder. Hell, while he'd been tossing and turning in his bed all night, Eva had probably spent her evening picking out a special jar for Walker's balls—clearly, she was about to take possession of them, and there wasn't a damn thing he could do about it. Not if he wanted to play again. Not if he wanted his contract renewed.

Coach had made that perfectly clear yesterday.

Last chance, Dunn. I'd hate to lose you, but we have to consider what's best for the whole team...

Walker sighed, then chugged the rest of his coffee,

enjoying the burn all the way down. Roscoe was right. No sense in calling it off. All he could do now was take his medicine like a man and hope to Christ she went a little easier on him today. Despite his macho talk yesterday, Walker didn't think his body could handle another workout as rigorous as that. Not that he'd ever admit that to anyone—not even to Roscoe or Henny, and especially not to the team docs. If they thought for one minute he was seriously hurting, they'd put him on disability faster than Henny's slapshot, and before he knew it, Walker would be all washed up, doing product endorsements and has-been celeb appearances at car dealerships and kids' parties. How long could he make a career out of that shit? How long could he cover his mother's expenses? His brothers' tuition bills? The house? All of it?

"Come on," Roscoe said, digging through the cupboard for a mug and helping himself to the rest of the coffee in the pot. "Get ready. Time for me to meet the woman who's gonna *own* you for the next six weeks."

"Hey Roscoe?" Walker asked, still not ready to be cheered up. "Anyone ever tell you to fuck off?"

"Once or twice."

"Well, just in case… fuck off. Oh, here's another one —fuck off—you can save it for later."

"I can't wait till your sorry ass is back on the ice. When you're not playing? You're kind of a douche." He punched Walker hard in the arm, and Walker finally cracked a smile, appreciating that simple word: *till*. It didn't occur to Roscoe that Walker *wouldn't* get better, that he wouldn't get back on the ice. For Roscoe, it was only a matter of time.

Maybe that bright side of his wasn't such a bad thing after all.

"Give me half an hour," Walker said. "I need a shower and some more food, then we'll head out."

"Better take care of yourself in there," Roscoe shouted down the hallway. "Don't want you embarrassing yourself with a raging hard-on in front of my future girlfriend."

"Hey Roscoe?"

"Yeah?"

Walker stuck his head out of the bathroom doorway, watching Roscoe dig through the cupboards for something to eat. He cracked up. "Fuck off."

In an effort to convince Walker that this shitshow was a good idea, McKellen had sent him a bunch of stats about Eva's qualifications last night. Turns out she really *was* a two-time Olympic medalist—they hadn't been yanking his chain about that. Half a bottle of Jim Beam into his pity party last night, Walker had even looked up some of

SYLVIA PIERCE

her routines on YouTube—wanted to know what he was dealing with.

Those videos were damn impressive.

But watching it on a laptop and seeing it up close and personal?

World of difference.

He and Roscoe stood just outside the locker room doorway, watching Eva own the ice, both of them completely dumbfounded.

"Holy shit." Roscoe nailed him in the arm. "You left out the part where she could do…um… *that*."

They both tilted their heads as Eva grabbed her ankle, lifting her leg above her head and gliding effortlessly around the rink. She really did look like something out of a music box—a ballerina on ice. They watched in silence as she continued through her routine, twirling and jumping, dancing across the ice so perfectly, Walker wondered whether her feet even touched the ground.

She slid toward the center ice, then turned into one of those spin moves that made Walker dizzy.

"Damn," Roscoe whispered.

"Just remember you're here to back me up, not to be a misogynistic asshole."

"Misogynistic? I'm just appreciating her exceptional—"

"Lock it down, thirty-eight." Walker clapped Roscoe hard on the shoulder, then turned back toward the ice.

Within seconds, he was completely mesmerized again, watching her move through a series of jumps, nailing every one. Anyone could see that she was technically good. Hell, she was incredible. But the way she moved out there was so much more than skill. More than training. More than talent and commitment and broken bones and all the three a.m. practices she'd probably endured as a kid, every single day for decades.

It was raw, unfiltered passion.

Yeah, the guys on the Tempest loved playing hockey. Tore it up on the ice, every single game, no matter what else was going on in their lives or how badly they were getting their asses kicked. But this was different. This was Eva, totally alone, lost in her own fucking beautiful world out there, skating for no other reason than the pure joy of it, and the sight of her stirred something in Walker that he hadn't felt in years.

Hell, maybe he'd never felt it. He certainly didn't know what the fuck to call it, that was for sure. All he knew was that right now, seeing that woman skate, seeing that look of pure bliss on her face, he wanted to be part of it. To know what she was all about.

She slid across the ice again, twirling into another spin, faster and faster until she was nothing more than a redheaded blur on the center ice.

And then she stopped. Just like that. One dainty toe pick against the ice, totally in control.

It felt like every molecule, every atom in that rink halted in an instant, the whole world going silent. If not for the white cloud of breath puffing out of her mouth, he might've thought she'd stopped breathing.

Walker certainly felt like *he* had.

He'd traveled all over the country, all over the world. Yet he could say with absolute certainty that Eva Bradshaw skating was the most beautiful thing he'd ever seen.

Walker sighed, his bad mood creeping back in. What the fuck was he even thinking? Women like that weren't for him. They were for the good guys, the undamaged guys, the ones who could promise her the world and fucking deliver. Not for guys like Walker. Guys who, no matter how many friends and teammates they had, no matter how many women offered up their company for the night, always woke up alone.

She was hired to do a job. And Walker had a job, too. Follow her instructions. Work through the pain in his knee. And get his ass back on the team. End of fucking story.

"Show's over," Walker said, trying to fight off the shiver he felt right down to his bones. He sat on the bench and hauled his skates out of the bag, ready to lace up and get his damn head in the game. "Time to work."

CHAPTER SEVEN

Eva glided across the empty ice, smoothed and buffed to a glassy sheen overnight, all evidence of yesterday's practice erased.

Holy snowballs, a girl could get used to this.

In her regular life, Eva made her living teaching people how to skate competitively—mostly kids, but also a handful of older teens and adults who'd gotten a late start on their dreams. Depending on the season, she spent anywhere from twenty to sixty hours a week on the ice, skating alongside her clients, demonstrating the jumps and combinations that had once made her semi-famous.

But it'd been a long time since she'd had an entire rink to herself—an entire, beautifully groomed, totally luxurious rink. Years, actually.

Gracie would love it, Eva thought. The girl wasn't

exactly following in her mom's footsteps when it came to competitive sports, but she definitely loved being out on the ice, sliding around, falling on her butt, being silly. Maybe they'd let her bring Gracie in on a weekend one day, just for a little while.

Eva sucked in a deep breath of crisp, icy air. She'd been here an hour already, and she only had a few more minutes of bliss before she had to meet Walker. Closing her eyes, she looped into a set of graceful figures on the ice, the swish-swish of the blades calming her in a way that only skating could. She moved by instinct, by feel, her skates an extension of her own body. Picking up speed, she glided down to the goal line, the chilly air snapping at her cheeks as she picked up speed, faster, faster still, launching into the air for a double axel/double toe loop combo jump, landing flawlessly.

God, what would it be like to get to do this every day?

She'd nearly forgotten how much she loved to skate. Just skate—no audience, no other responsibilities, no anxious parents shouting from the sidelines as Eva tried to mold their children into future Olympians.

Eva smiled. It wasn't often she could indulge like this.

And you can't today, either. Walker Dunn—remember?

Eva wobbled on her skates, her serenity interrupted by memories of her time with Walker yesterday. Her blood still boiled with anger and frustration at how hard-headed he'd been, how cocky and cold. Didn't he realize how many people were trying to help him?

No matter. All she could do was try to teach him her techniques. The bad attitude? That was for his coaches to tackle. Eva would *not* let Walker scare her off—not with that potentially life-changing job offer on the line.

Eva looped through a figure eight, pushing herself harder and faster, then leaned forward, raising her leg high above her head, gliding into an arabesque spiral, her thoughts emptying of everything but here, but now, but the cold air on her cheeks, the ice beneath her blades.

When she reached the center ice, she arched into a seamless layback spin, keeping her eyes open this time, her head thrown back, the colors of the rink blurring like watercolors until Eva wasn't sure where she stopped and the rest of the world began.

And then, when she was ready, she slowly rose to her full height, placed her toe pick against the ice, and stopped.

The world came back to her slowly, one sense at a time. First the sound of her breathing, the feel of her breath whooshing in and out of her lungs. Then the bright red seats and polished mahogany benches of the arena, sharpening into focus. The crisp, slightly chlorinated taste of the air. The whir of the ice machines below.

And there, at the other end of the rink, Walker Dunn, heading right for her.

She wondered how long he'd been watching her, whether he'd seen her nail those jumps. The idea sent a little jolt of excitement through her nerves, and as his mouth hitched into a crooked grin, her first instinct was to smile back.

But... no. She couldn't allow herself to warm up to him. Couldn't expose her heart, even for a casual friendship. The risks were too great. She would never, ever put herself through that kind of hurt again. Never end up broken on the kitchen floor, sobbing and afraid, wishing she could hit the rewind button on her whole life.

She wasn't a reckless, impulsive teenager anymore. She was a mother. A *single* mother with the sole responsibility for keeping another human being alive, for nurturing that sweet little human into adulthood. Gracie came first, full stop. And that meant Eva had to keep very clear, very solid boundaries between her work life and personal life, no matter how much Walker had secretly intrigued her, no matter how bright that flame of attraction flickered inside her. It just wasn't happening. Not with Walker. Not with anyone.

If that made her a cold-hearted bitch in the eyes of everyone around her, so be it. She'd rather be cold-hearted than *broken*-hearted, even if it meant being alone.

At least when you were alone, no one could break your heart but you.

"You're early," she said, forcing some ice into her voice.

Yeah, that's me! Stone-cold Eva Bradshaw. Watch out, world!

"Had I known you'd be doing a show, I would've been a hell of a lot earlier." Walker's gaze swept her face, trailed slowly down her body, then back up. Through another cocky grin, he said, "Pretty sweet moves, princess. I'll give you that."

He was blatantly flirting with her, but she didn't know if he was just screwing around, or if he was feeling the same sparks of attraction that were currently setting off little fires in her belly.

Again, she bit back her smile.

What is wrong with you? You're an Olympic champion, not some schoolgirl with a crush. Pull it together!

Eva squared her shoulders and held his gaze. "How's the knee today, old dog?"

"Holding up just fine." He flexed it a bit. "It'll take more than one night with you to knock me down."

"Who's your friend?" Eva nodded behind Walker as another man approached, broad-shouldered and sexy—God, they were practically a matched set. But where Walker was guarded and cocky, this man smiled openly, his demeanor loose and carefree.

"Evangeline Bradshaw," Walker said, "meet Roscoe LeGrand. He's my left winger."

"And an excellent cook," Roscoe said, shaking her hand. "How do you feel about Italian? When you're done mopping the ice with my boy here, maybe we could go back to my place and—"

"Ah, Roscoe. Such a kidder, this guy." Walker clamped his hand down over Roscoe's shoulder. "He's here to help. I asked him to video the session, give me some pointers later."

"Fair enough," she said. "As long as he doesn't get in the way."

"He won't," Walker said. "Not if he knows what's good for him."

Is he... jealous?

That spark zinged through Eva's nervous system again, making her cheeks go hot. She resisted the urge to unzip her fleece. As far as she was concerned, the more layers between her and Walker, the better.

"I'll be over here," Roscoe said, skating off to the side. "Not getting in the way. Unless you change your mind and want me in the middle, or on top—"

"Roscoe?"

"Wait, don't tell me... fuck off?"

Both men laughed, and this time, Eva couldn't hold back her smile. The mood was instantly lighter; seeing Walker joke around with one of his friends had humanized him a bit. Reminded her that he really *was* just a man, after all, just like she'd told her sister yesterday in the locker room. Not some impossibly unreachable hockey god who'd descended down from the sky just to become her complete undoing.

"Ready to work, forty-six?" Eva asked.

"Ready to *be* worked, you mean?"

"Yes, that."

Walker nodded, returning her smile as he pulled on his helmet and fastened the chinstrap. "I'm all yours, princess. Let's do it."

CHAPTER EIGHT

Death by ball-busting.

Maybe it didn't exist, but Walker was pretty sure that's what was going on his death certificate when they wheeled his ass into the morgue later.

Eva crossed her arms in front of her chest, clipboard dangling from one hand, her eyes tracking Walker's every move. She had him powering through a line of orange cones without lifting his skates off the ice, trying to harness energy from shifting his weight back and forth. Physics, as she loved to keep reminding him.

It was working. Maybe. But Walker's knee didn't like it a bit. Each time he took the weight back to his right side, his joints protested.

"Is your knee holding up okay?" she called out across the ice.

"Just fine," he called back, trying not to grit his teeth.

"No sharp pain?" She skated up close. Despite her all-business tone, there was concern in her eyes, a softness that would've made him melt if he still had a heart beating in that empty chest of his. "No swelling or pressure?"

"I said it's fine."

"Okay. Let's try another drill, then." She glanced at her clipboard, scribbled something with the pen chained to the top. "Inside and outside edges. Ready?"

Fuck. Far as his knee was concerned, that was the worst drill. Worse than the forward strides. The c-cuts. The slalom. The running crossovers. The mohawk turns. She'd been running him through the gauntlet, familiar hockey moves tweaked with her own figure skating twists, and Walker was struggling to keep up.

Despite his best efforts to keep his discomfort on lockdown, Eva seemed to sense his hesitation.

"We can break any time you want to," she said.

"Nah, I'm good." Ignoring the pain, Walker pushed ahead, propelling down the rink as he shifted back and forth between the outside and inside edges of his blades. It felt like rocking on butter knives, and now *both* his knees were grumbling.

"Trust your edges, Walker!" she called out.

"Okay!" he shouted, biting back the urge to add,

"Mom." The thought made him smile, just for a minute. His own mother had been his number one supporter from the start and had done her fair share of shouting at him from the sidelines—even after he'd been drafted into the NHL. Walker figured she'd earned it, though.

She'd scraped together every penny, hiding half of the tips she'd earned from two different waitressing jobs in a box of tampons under the bathroom sink just to keep his father from stealing it for booze. She'd paid for Walker's hockey lessons with that money, standing up to his father during the man's worst rages.

Up until she got sick, she'd never missed a game. But two seasons ago, her doctor worried that the games were too disorienting for her. The noise, the flashes, the people. She'd come home confused and scared more often than not, and Walker wouldn't put her through that again—not even if he *could* play.

He hadn't decided what—if anything—to tell her about Eva.

Mom would love her.

Shaking off the ridiculous thought, Walker skated to the net at the other end of the rink and paused for a breather. He crouched down to retie his laces—a stall tactic—but Eva was already shouting orders again.

"Now, I want you to skate back toward me," she said. "Same drill, but see if you can pick up the pace a little. Ready?"

He caught Roscoe's eye from the penalty box and rolled his eyes, but there was no solidarity to be found there. Roscoe just grinned and gave him the thumbs up, holding up his video camera to capture the moves.

Fucking traitor.

Taking a deep breath, Walker stood up and shot back across the ice, shifting his weight between the inside and outside edges of his blades, just like she'd instructed.

"That was better," she said when he'd reached the net on Eva's side. "But your right leg is still holding you back. Look—watch me."

She slid across the ice in front of him, rocking on her blades, easy as pie. Turning to look at him over her shoulder, she said, "You're not bending in enough on that inside edge—see?" She did it again, barely breaking a sweat. "This move should help you, but the way you're doing it, it's costing you time and energy. I want you to try again, but this time focus on—"

"Got it. Thanks." He zoomed back around for another go, determined—for some twisted reason—to please her. To prove that he could handle anything she threw at him. He got down to the opposite net, but before he made it back, she was skating toward him, shaking her head.

"No, no, no," she said, exasperated. She slid to a stop in front of him, her eyes narrowed, one hand on her hip, the other still clutching that damn clipboard. "Walker. You need a break."

"And you know that because... you're in my head? I don't think so, princess."

Her eyes sparked with fire, just like they had yesterday. "You tell me your knee is holding up, yet—"

"It *is* holding up."

"—*yet* your right leg is dragging. You're favoring it on every turn. You can't pivot properly, your hips are way too tight, you've got limited range of motion, those edges are a hot mess, and—"

"Jesus." Walker barked out a dry laugh. "Why don't you tell me how you *really* feel?"

Her eyes widened, nostrils flaring. The tips of her ears turned bright red, and Walker bit back a smile—a real one. Damn, he liked seeing her all riled up. Liked that he was the one pushing her buttons.

"How I *feel* is irrelevant," she said. "What I'm *observing*—from one professional to another—is that you are completely full of shit." Her gaze flicked to his knee, then back up again. "And if you don't start owning up to it, you're going to delay your recovery, or worse—do permanent damage to your body. So instead of sulking like an overgrown baby, maybe you should—"

"Maybe I should what? Do a few more twirls and loop-de-loops for you? Dance like a trained monkey while you stand on the sidelines thinking up new ways to torture me?" Yeah, he knew her moves were supposed to help him, but the more time he spent out here on the ice with her, the more ridiculous he felt. He didn't need skating lessons. He needed a new knee. And despite Eva's many talents, he was pretty sure she couldn't help him with that.

"You've got to give this stuff a chance," she said. "You'll get there—it just takes some time to learn my methods. To *unlearn* some of that hockey training that's holding you back."

"Unlearn the training that got me to the NHL? Hard pass, princess. And for your information, the knee is just fine. Go ahead and write that on your little clipboard."

"Are you even listening to yourself?" Without warning, she cocked her arm back and winged that clipboard across the ice so hard it slid into the boards with a clatter.

Wow, Walker hadn't seen that coming. She was seriously pissed.

Walker blew out a breath. "Eva, take it easy. I'm—"

"Don't tell me to take it easy, forty-six. Your job is on the line. You're fucking around out here, cocky as hell, insulting me, lying about your injury, and meanwhile, your whole career is about to slide into the gutter."

"You *are* the expert there, aren't you?" he spat.

Shit.

He hadn't meant it. It was just a nasty little barb that had come into his head and fallen out of his big, dumb mouth, totally unfiltered.

A flicker of hurt passed through her eyes, and Walker's gut twisted. He didn't know why she'd left the Olympic track—couldn't really find much about it online. Just that she'd gone to the games twice, kicked ass, and everyone thought she'd be back for a third round, but it didn't happen. The media eventually lost interest, Eva got into coaching or whatever else she did now, and that was it.

But that wounded look in her eyes... *damn*. Whatever had happened back then, it obviously hadn't been easy on her. It was probably still an open wound, and he'd just poured some salt in it.

You fucking piece of shit.

"Eva... shit." He skated closer, reached out to touch her shoulder. She pulled back immediately, that wounded look in her eyes evaporating, replaced by the icy, untouchable gaze she seemed to keep on speed-dial, just for him.

"Eva. I didn't mean—"

"Let's get something straight, asshole," she snapped. "I don't care what you think of me and my life choices. I'm not here to be your friend, or your mama, or your nanny, or your damn wet nurse."

Walker's brain was instantly invaded by an image of Eva straddling him in his bed, those perfect tits in his face, his tongue licking her nipples, sucking her, making up for every rotten thing he'd said, one stroke at a time...

Jesus, you really are an asshole...

"I'm here to get you back on your team before your bosses cut your ass loose," she said, bringing him right back to the moment. She slid the phone out of her fleece pocket and held it between them. "So if we've got different goals here, let's call up McKellen right now and let him know the deal's off. I'm sure we can both find something better to do with our time."

He could think of about *twenty* better things he'd like to do with her time. And yeah, maybe he was acting like a first-rate cocksucker, but he wouldn't even be *thinking* about those things if he hadn't picked up the same hot, carnal, totally turned-on vibe from her. It was pretty obvious they couldn't stand each other, but hot damn, were they down to fuck. Walker knew how *he* felt, and one look at *her*—those dilated pupils, her chest heaving, her neck and cheeks flush.... He'd pissed her off, sure. But there was a lot more going on there than just anger.

It was lust. Pure and simple.

Eva stared at him. Hard. Her breathing was uneven, her lips parted, hands on her hips. She slid a step closer again, her eyes raking him over, up and down, finally settling on his mouth. Their bodies were so close, he could feel her hot, ragged breath on his cheeks, could see the little divot just beneath her bottom lip, the tiny freckle that sat at the corner of her mouth, darker than the ones sprinkled across her nose.

He wanted to kiss it. To taste her soft skin, to slide his tongue between those lips and feel her hot little mouth.

Her tongue darted out to wet her lips, almost involuntarily, and Walker's dick strained hard against his pants. In that moment, no one could convince him that he and Eva weren't sharing the same base, primal thought—what they'd do to each other naked, rolling around on the floor like animals, hot and wet and hard and angry as fuck.

The tension was so thick, so hot, Walker wanted to explode.

He reached for her, clamped his big hand around hers, the phone gripped firmly between them. "I think our goals are pretty much right in alignment, princess."

"Yeah? You think so?" Her voice was soft now, almost a whisper, but the charge was still there, white-hot and electric. Walker lifted his hand to her face, brushed his thumb across her lower lip. Eva gasped, parting her lips as her velvet tongue slid along the tip of his thumb, urging him deeper into her lush mouth, her teeth grazing his knuckle.

She's gonna make me come. Right here. Just like this.

Eva bit the tip of his thumb, and Walker groaned, his free hand sliding down on her hip, urging her closer...

"Aaaaand... cut!" A voice shouted from the penalty box, followed by raucous laughter.

It was like a gallon of ice water directly to the balls.

Roscoe was doubling over in the box, Henny shaking his head beside him, the two of them damn near pissing their pants with laughter.

Walker slid his thumb out of her mouth, and Eva backed away, her cheeks flushed.

Walker's dick instantly shriveled. He'd fucking forgot Roscoe was even there. Videoing the whole damn fight, no less. And when the fuck had Henny shown up?

Walker's head was spinning. His thumb was still wet from where Eva had sucked on him, a cold reminder that her sweet, hot mouth was no longer anywhere near him.

A travesty of epic proportions.

Roscoe pointed at his camera. "Sorry, did you want me to keep filming? Maybe try another angle? I could— no? Okay. Carry on, then."

Douche bag.

Walker sighed. Roscoe and Henny lacked finesse, but they'd never done or said anything that wasn't in Walker's best interest, even if it sucked ass. The boys were right to interrupt. That was a close fucking call.

Walker might not like the idea of taking hockey lessons from an ice princess, but if McKellen found out he'd fucked the whole thing up with sex, they'd probably tear up his contract right there.

Despite the attitude he'd thrown at Eva, Walker did *not* want to be out on the street.

Eva had skated over to retrieve her clipboard, and

now she was back, her shoulders set, her chin tilted up, lips pressed together, completely closed off. It was as if he'd imagined the scorching heat between them—as if it'd never even happened.

"So." Walker's voice broke. He cleared his throat, kicking at the ice with his skate. "We should probably…."

"Yeah," she said, blowing out a breath.

Walker nodded, not knowing what else to say. He didn't do this—this post-almost-but-not-quite-hooking-up awkward as fuck conversation. Hell, he'd never even been in a situation like that before with a woman. He'd never *not* sealed the deal after a moment like that.

Be real, dickhead. You've never even come close to a moment like that.

Walker sucked in a breath of icy air, trying to slow down his heart, still hammering away in his chest. Sure, he'd had some good times, got downright dirty with plenty of women on the road, back before his injury. But that's all they were—fun times. Hot sex.

Eva? They hadn't even kissed. He hadn't touched more than her soft mouth, yet he couldn't remember anything so damn erotic in his life. So perfect. Everything in him was wound up tight, his head fuzzy, his mouth still watering for the taste of her he hadn't gotten.

With one touch, one breath, Eva had gotten completely under his skin.

"We should definitely not—" She blew out a breath and slicked her hair back, even though not a strand was out of place. "—do that again. Ever."

Was it possible that his dick could shrink even more?

"Good call," he said, pointing at her. Then, making a show of wiping imaginary sweat off his brow, "Whew! Dodged that bullet."

Neither of them spoke.

"Awkward," she whispered, lowering her eyes.

"Little bit, yeah."

Eva skated backward away from him, shaking out her arms. "Can we just… erase the last fifteen minutes?"

"By skating backward and shaking?" He imitated her move, exaggerating the swish in his hips. "Is this some figure skater time travel trick?"

Eva laughed. She fucking laughed, and damn if Walker didn't light up like a Christmas tree.

He picked up a little speed, gliding past her toward the net. "How fast do I have to skate to go back, say, ten years? Because if you think I'm bad now… Jesus. I was a *serious* asshole back then, and there's some shit I could probably stand to fix."

"Sure. Maybe if we get through a few drills without killing each other, I'll teach you the time travel move." Eva was cracking up again, the tension between them evaporating as she fell in line next to him, skating along the goal line. When they reached the boards, they both stopped, and Eva turned to face him, holding out her hand to shake. "Do we have a deal, forty-six?"

She was still smiling, but Walker knew it wasn't a joke. Something between them had shifted, and her handshake was a peace offering. A do-over. Didn't stop the ache in his balls, or chase away the disappointment in his gut that he hadn't been able to taste her sweet mouth, but it definitely cleared the air between them.

He grabbed her delicate hand, which was soft and warm and a hell of a lot stronger than it looked. "You got yourself a deal, Evangeline."

Her eyes darkened, and she immediately lowered her gaze, a new blush creeping into her skin. "No more princess, huh?"

Before he could respond, Eva looked up at him again, thoughtful. "Look, Walker... I'm pushing you hard out here because I know you can handle it. I see you struggling with that injury, but I *know* you can do this." She put a warm hand on his shoulder, her eyes soft and unguarded for the first time since they'd met. Fuck, he wanted to fall right into them, forget about the rink and Roscoe and Henny and his aching bones and just totally fucking lose himself in this woman. "You're doing a great job, despite our... our challenges. I mean it."

"Yeah?" He couldn't hide the smile on his face, the rush of pleasure in his chest that she'd actually complimented him. Every muscle in his body was ready to revolt, and Walker had considered it a win that he'd managed to keep himself upright the whole time, but Eva had said he'd done great. Great!

He was still smiling.

"So, I think we can call it a day, start fresh again tomorrow. Okay?" she asked.

"You got it, princess."

Now it was her turn for a smile.

Walker didn't say anything else, just watched her skate away and hop out of the rink, his knee throbbing, dick still at half-mast.

Despite their sparring, the chemistry between them was off the charts—and that was just on the ice. He could only imagine what they'd be like together in bed. But that's as far as Walker was letting it go—his imagination. Maybe a fantasy or two to get him through those frigid Buffalo winter nights. Today had been a fluke—a momentary lapse in judgment. It wouldn't—couldn't—happen again.

Thing was, he was starting to fucking *like* her. Really like her. And it pissed him off.

Walker waited until she was out of the arena before he sat down on the players' bench to strip off his skates.

"Well," Henny said, laughing. "She's fucking *hot*. And hardcore as hell. And hot. Did I mention hot? I like her."

"Sure you do. Hey, thanks again for the cockblock,

bro." Walker's tone dripped with sarcasm, even though he was actually relieved they'd interrupted him. "Definitely made the right call there."

"We saved your stupid ass from self-destruction," Henny said. "You *should* be thanking us, asswipe."

"I know." Walker shook his head, then nodded at the camera. To Roscoe, he said, "Other than your homemade porno, did you get any decent footage on the ice?"

"Got it all," Roscoe said. "*Including* the porno."

"Yeah, I'm gonna need a copy of that, by the way," Henny said.

Walker clipped them both on the back of their rock-solid heads. "How'd I look out there?"

"You looked good," Roscoe said, shrugging. "Made it through all the drills, didn't wipe out, didn't cry too hard when she cracked the whip."

"I like when a woman cracks the whip." Henny grinned.

"And?" Walker held out his arms, waiting for something useful. He needed pointers about his technique, not bullshit jokes. "What do you guys *think*?"

"I think, sir," Roscoe said, still laughing, "that you are in a fuck lot of trouble with this woman."

"Seconded," said Henny.

"You're thinking with your dick," said Roscoe.

"Never a good idea," said Henny. Then, with a predatory smile, "But if you're gonna go down in flames over a woman, your ice princess is worth the burn."

Don't I fucking know it, bro. Don't I fucking know it.

CHAPTER NINE

"No chance you can play hooky, huh?" Marybeth asked as they pulled up to the front of the ice rink.

"Don't tempt me." Eva turned around in the passenger seat to look at Gracie, all smiles in her frilly white dress, red-and-white striped tights, and a Santa hat she'd adorned with rainbow sequins. Marybeth was taking her to Breakfast with Santa and the Elves at the Galleria Mall today; the kid had stayed up half the night putting together the perfect outfit.

Eva sighed. It was only a couple of days into December, but the schools were closed today for budget meetings, everyone already half checked out for the holidays. Eva's workload usually picked up in December, but she'd always been able to do the breakfast, photos with Santa, the Festival of Lights parade, and anything else Gracie loved doing this time of year.

But all that was strictly BW—before Walker.

Thank God for Aunt Marybeth.

"I'll be finished this afternoon," Eva told Gracie. "Then we've got the whole rest of the weekend together. Okay?"

Gracie beamed. "Don't worry, Mama. I'll tell Santa what you want for Christmas."

"I'd appreciate it." Eva winked and turned back to her sister, her heart heavy with guilt.

"You'll be done before you know it," Marybeth said. "We'll be back to pick you up at one-thirty."

"Better make it two." Eva flipped down the visor and peeked in the mirror, repositioning an errant bobby pin that had slipped out of her bun. "Walker can be a bit... unpredictable."

'Unpredictable' was putting it mildly. Their last session had started out okay—they'd joked around, managed to sidestep most of the lingering awkwardness from their almost-kiss, got in a pretty great workout on the ice. But the hours that followed had been rocky, with Walker getting frustrated at the more challenging drills, and Eva snapping at him in retaliation. They'd ended up arguing straight through the last half of practice.

Because if we didn't fight, we'd probably end up in bed together.

Eva dismissed the thought, shoving it way down inside where it would hopefully remain, at least for the next few hours. It was bad enough she was losing sleep over the man, her nights consumed with that single, red-hot memory, replaying every moment: the intense desire in his eyes, even as they flashed with anger. The feel of his skin, the rough pad of his thumb sliding between her lips, the salty taste of him on her tongue. The low, barely audible growl that had escaped from his throat the moment her lips parted... she'd felt it more than heard it, and her whole body had reacted, heart hammering in her chest as molten desire flooded her core.

She wondered if Walker had any idea how much that forbidden moment had affected her.

"You okay?" Marybeth tapped Eva's thigh, her brow furrowed in concern. "You're a million miles away over there."

"Just... just thinking about my job. Like I said, he's kind of unpredictable."

"I'm sure you can handle it," Marybeth said.

"I hope you're right." Eva's ridiculous sex-starved fantasies aside, she needed Walker to start making tangible progress. Every hour that passed without significant improvements on his times, his chances at getting back on the team dwindled—along with her chances at scoring that full-time position. McKellen had asked her to think about it, and she'd taken that to heart. Other than Walker, who'd been sneaking into her thoughts a lot more often than she wanted to admit, that job was at the top of Eva's mind. The more she thought about it, the more it began to feel like the right move. She'd even started browsing online for apartments and elementary schools in Saint Paul, just trying to get a feel for the area.

Her eyes misted, blurring her reflection in the visor mirror. She hadn't told Marybeth or Gracie about the offer yet—no use getting anyone excited, worried, or otherwise worked up about a move to Minnesota unless it was a solid possibility. And right now, without Walker's cooperation, it was just another dream about to pass right on by.

Eva flipped the visor up, blinking away her tears. "He doesn't trust me. Every time I think we've made some progress, he shuts down again."

"Do *you* trust *him*?"

"Irrelevant. I'm not the one who needs coaching."

"I don't know. I think it needs to go both ways. It's like any relationship—"

"We're not in a relationship."

Marybeth raised a curious eyebrow. "Oh my God. Don't tell me..." She pointed an accusatory finger at Eva's chest. Lowering her voice, she said, "You've got a crush on the hockey man!"

"There's no crush. I'm just—"

"I can't believe you!" Marybeth's eyes were wide with shock, but a smile played at the corners of her mouth. "We talked about this, Eva. After everything that happened with—"

"It's *soooo* not like that," Eva said. "Trust me."

"Is the hockey man coming to help decorate our tree tonight?" Gracie piped up from the back.

"No, honeybee," Eva said firmly. "The hockey man is *not* coming."

Marybeth snorted. "Poor hockey man."

Eva smacked her, but she was laughing now, too. "Stop!"

"Aunt Marybeth said we could make popcorn gardens for the tree," Gracie said.

Marybeth laughed. "Garlands, sweet pea."

"That sounds... great," Eva said. In a low voice that only Marybeth could hear, she said, "I'm sure the mice will appreciate them."

"You worry too much," Marybeth said, her easy, care-free laughter filling the car.

Eva couldn't argue with that. She worried about everything—whether Gracie was making friends at school, whether she'd be able to pay the electric *and* the gas bill this month, whether her mother would show up unannounced just to remind Eva of all the ways she was failing Gracie as a mother.

And now she worried about Walker. About screwing up her shot at this job.

"Hey," Marybeth said, her tone suddenly soft. "You'll

figure out how to get through to him. Maybe you're going too easy on him."

"He's injured. He can't risk more complications—it could mean the end of his career."

"I'm talking about the mental part," Marybeth said. "You don't take shit—"

"You can't say shit!" Gracie said. "Santa will put you on the naughty list."

Eva giggled. "You tell her, Gracie."

"Stuff," Marybeth continued. "You don't take stuff from your other students, so don't take it from him."

"He's an NHL superstar," Eva said, rolling her eyes. "He is, as they say, a pretty big deal around here."

"All the more reason he probably needs his butt kicked. Anyway, if anyone can get through to him, you can. I've seen you shut down a rink full of cranky toddlers like a *boss*."

Eva smiled at her sister's confidence in her, but as she stared out the windshield at the doors that led into the arena, she felt a tightness in her chest, a bubbling in her stomach. Walker was *worse* than a cranky toddler. He was a cranky *man*—impossible, pig-headed... and yeah. So damn sexy she could hardly concentrate on their work. Every time she sent him down the ice, she'd start imagining him naked, imagining what it would be like if those strong muscles were flexing and pumping like that for her, imagining how it would feel to run her tongue along the ridges of his rock-hard abs...

"Speak of the devil... isn't that your man?" Marybeth nodded toward the passenger side window, and Eva whipped her head around to see. Through the white fog of Marybeth's car exhaust, she saw Walker striding across the parking lot toward the rink, gear bag slung over his shoulder, a blue-and-silver Buffalo Tempest knit hat pulled down over his messy hair. The sun glinted off his dark shades, his breath puffing out in front of him— the man was a vision of utter hotness on an otherwise frigid morning. His very presence did more to wake up Eva's body than the two cups of coffee she'd chugged earlier.

Not that Marybeth needed to know about *that*.

Marybeth leaned into Eva's seat to get a closer look out the window. "So that's Walker Dunn, huh?"

"The one and only," Eva said, just as his head turned in their direction. She didn't think he noticed her, though.

"Can we meet him?" Marybeth asked.

"Yeah, Mama!" Gracie exclaimed. "Can we meet the hockey man?"

"No," Eva said. She turned to look at Gracie again. "I'm sorry. Mr. Dunn is kind of... he's..." God, her brain was freezing up, and Walker was getting closer, and if either Marybeth or Gracie knocked on the window or opened the door, there was no way he wouldn't see…

"He's socially awkward," Eva blurted out. "Issues. He has issues. Doesn't like people. Um, people bothering him. He's very… private."

Oh my God, shut up!

Marybeth cracked up. "Nice save, and by the way, you are so full of it, and by the way, we are *so* talking about this later."

Eva gritted her teeth, plastering on a smile. "There is nothing to talk about."

"Maybe he wants to come with us to meet Santa," Gracie offered.

"That's very sweet of you," Marybeth said. "But I think Mr. Dunn is busy working with Mommy today. Maybe another time."

Over my dead body.

There would never be another time. The last thing she needed was Gracie getting her heart crushed just because Walker was in a shit mood or didn't like kids.

A little stab of pain pricked her heart at the thought, but she shut it down. For one thing, she had no idea whether he liked kids. For all she knew, he might even have his own kids—kids that he loved and adored and spoiled rotten. And for another thing, it didn't matter. Not a bit. Because no matter what her own ridiculous, cavewoman, purely physical feelings about Walker were, that had nothing to do with her daughter. She would never, ever expose Gracie to Walker, or to *any* hockey player, for that matter.

"See you girls later," Eva said, grabbing her bag from the floor and blowing kisses to them both. "Have fun with the elves!"

She flung herself out of the car, slammed the door shut behind her, and bolted for the entrance.

"Allow me," a deep, gravelly voice called out from behind her. Of course it was him.

She stepped aside and let him grab the door, grateful that Marybeth was already zooming out of the lot.

"Carpool day?" he asked, following her line of sight.

"Something like that."

"I could've picked you up, princess."

She returned his teasing grin and walked through the doorway, ignoring the heat in her belly as her arm brushed against his stomach. God, he smelled delicious. Like soap and mint and wood smoke and—*gah*—man. Hot, impossibly sexy man.

"Then I'd have to tell you where I live," she said, "and obviously that's not happening."

"Hmm. Afraid I might show up unannounced? Give the neighbors something to talk about?"

The door clicked shut behind them, and Eva picked up the pace, walking down the long corridor that led to the locker rooms. No way she'd let him see that blush on her face. No way she'd give him the satisfaction of knowing he'd put it there.

Still, his legs were long and powerful, and he was already there, *right* behind her.

"Thanks for the offer," she said softly, her eyes fixed on the ground in front of her. "But I don't need a ride."

"You don't *need* a ride." His voice was low and sexy, his breath hot on the back of her exposed neck. "But maybe you'd *like* it."

"A... a ride?"

"Yes, Evangeline. A ride." His scent enveloped her again, the warmth from his body radiating against her back.

She knew exactly what he was offering now, and it had nothing to do with carpooling. It was the first time he'd given her such an obvious entry, an invitation to pick up where they'd left off the other day.

"No friends today?" she asked, struggling to keep the tremble from her voice.

"Just us today, princess. Does that bother you?"

Eva shivered. Roscoe and Henny had shown up again last time, taking notes and cheering him on from the bench. Eva didn't mind—she'd liked their camaraderie, their obvious concern for Walker. She wished they were here again now, but for totally different reasons.

She and Walker were alone here, this particular arena booked solely for them. With obligations to the rest of the team elsewhere in the city, McKellen and Gallagher had left Walker entirely in Eva's hands. Which meant that if she went along with this right here, right now, no one would know. She could drop her bag, follow him into the locker room, strip off her clothes, let him wrap his big, strong hands around her hips and—

No. No way.

Eva closed her eyes, trying to steady her breathing. She let Walker's words hang unanswered in the air behind her, refusing to turn around, refusing to acknowledge the sparks crackling between them. He was stripping her of all resistance. One more minute with him, one more utterance, one more breath and she might just give herself over completely.

But no matter how insanely attracted to him she felt, no matter how riled up he made her, Eva couldn't allow herself to go there. There were walls around her heart for a reason, and she needed them to stay firmly in place.

"Playtime is over, forty-six," she said, hefting her bag over her shoulder and pushing the locker room door open. "We've got a lot of ground to cover today, and the clock's already ticking. I want you geared up and on the ice in ten, ready to work."

She still couldn't look at him. Not yet.

One heartbeat.

Grab me by the shoulders, Walker.

Two.

Spin me around.

Three.

Push me up against that wall. Hard.

Four.

And kiss me like you damn well mean it.

Five.

"Yes, ma'am," Walker said, his voice back to neutral. "See you on the ice, princess."

When Eva heard his footsteps heading down toward the men's locker room, she blew out a breath and opened her eyes, turning to watch his retreating form.

Her sister was—as usual—right.

Eva was *seriously* crushing on the hockey man.

CHAPTER TEN

"Faster, forty-six. Push it. Push it. *Push it*!" Eva shouted across the rink, stopwatch in one hand, clipboard in the other, watching Walker zoom through the cones. He was skating with the stick and puck today, and doing a pretty kickass job. He'd made it through every drill she'd set up for him so far, no slip-ups, no complaints, and—despite the post-flirting awkwardness that was getting to be a regular thing with them—he seemed in good spirits.

Unfortunately, his times still weren't where they needed to be. Getting closer, but not close enough. He was nailing the moves she'd taught him, so in theory he should've been picking up more speed, but it just wasn't happening.

"Clean up those edges and haul ass!" she shouted again. "Come on, forty-six! Show me what you're made of!"

Walker pushed himself harder, racing down the rink toward the net, never letting the puck escape his control. In a move that happened so fast Eva didn't even see it coming, he slapped the puck into the net.

"He shoots, he scores!" Walker raised both hands in the air, pumping his stick up and down. "And the crowd goes wild."

Eva let out a whoop and skated over to him.

"Was that your version of wild?" Walker laughed. "We need to work on that."

They fell into an easy glide, cooling down with a few laps around the rink.

"You ever been to a game?" he asked.

Eva's stomach knotted up. "Not… not in years."

"Guess we need to work on that, too. You should come with me some time. We can sit up in the exec suite, eat twenty dollar hotdogs, drink Roscoe and Henny under the table at the after party."

Eva forced a smile, wishing she could say it sounded like fun. Wishing she could take him up on it. Wishing some part of her still liked hockey games.

As a kid, she'd loved going to the games with her father—high up in the cheap seats, the nosebleeds, they'd eat popcorn and cheer for the Tempest, going home hoarse and happy no matter who'd won. Marybeth had never liked going, so it became a tradition for

Eva and her father alone, something that bonded them, just like her figure skating had.

But several years ago, Eva had gone to a game with her skating team as part of a fundraiser for Children's Hospital—Buffalo Tempest versus the Seattle Vipers. With a flush of heat, she realized now that Walker must've been playing that night, but she didn't know him then. After all, Walker wasn't the one who'd talked her up at the after party. The one who'd said all the right things, made all the right moves. The one who was full of promises.

The one who didn't show his true colors until the night Eva found out she was pregnant.

That guy played for the Vipers, but it didn't matter. He'd ruined hockey for her. The games. The players. The only thing she trusted now was this job, and that was only because McKellen had put his money where his mouth was.

Trying to keep the mood light, Eva nudged Walker in the ribs. "I think you should focus less on hotdogs and more on your times."

He skidded to a stop and looked at her full on. His face pinched with concern, with frustration. "You're telling me I'm still not close? How is that even possible?"

"You're closer, but you've still got a ways to go, Walker." Eva resisted the urge to smooth the angry wrinkle between his eyes. "Hey. We're only a few sessions in. We'll get there."

She held his gaze, willing him to believe it. Willing herself to believe it. Yeah, they still had weeks to work on it. But the prickly feeling in her gut told her that Walker was already pushing his limits on the ice.

"Walker, I need you to be honest with me about something," she said. Walker nodded, and she pressed on. "How much pain are you in right now?"

He winced at her question as if the words themselves were the cause of the injury. "I made the shot. That's what you wanted, right?"

"Think you could make that shot in front of twenty thousand screaming fans, lights flashing everywhere you look, two or three guys on your ass and a goalie in front of the net?"

"*You're* on my ass, princess. Might as well be three guys." He skated away from her, heading back for the net and scooping up the puck.

She gave him space, hoping another shot at the net would calm him, open him up to talking about it. But instead of skating down the rink, he grabbed up his stuff and headed for the players' bench.

Damn.

She followed him, stepping off the ice and straddling the wide mahogany bench so she could face him. Her knees brushed against his thigh, but he didn't flinch.

Eva ignored the heat between them. "Walker. Look at me. Please."

After a beat, he finally acquiesced. The hurt in his eyes was so plain it made her heart ache.

"What aren't you telling me?" she asked softly.

"Trust me, princess." Walker forced a laugh, pinning her again with a fiery glare. The hurt she'd seen in his eyes was hidden once again. "You *really* don't want me to answer that."

"Be serious. Five minutes, that's all I'm asking."

Walker pinched the bridge of his nose and closed his eyes, but he nodded. "You've got eyes, Eva. You know what's going on."

"You're in pain."

"Does it matter? Pain or not, I need to get back on the team, or I'm kinda fucked."

"Destroy your knee, and you're *totally* fucked."

Walker blew out a frustrated breath. "You don't understand."

"Understand what? You shut down every time I ask a question." Eva yanked off her gloves and tossed them onto the bench, barely keeping her temper in check. No matter how much progress they made, she still felt Walker pushing back at every turn. He was resisting her, holding himself back, keeping her at arm's length.

She wanted to help him, but he wouldn't let her in.

"How bad do you want this, Walker? Honestly. How damn bad do you want this?"

Walker yanked off his helmet and shoved a hand through his messy hair. "What do you think, princess?"

"I don't know what to think. From where I stand, I don't see a guy who's got his head in the game. I see a guy who's going through the motions. Trying to prove something to everyone but himself."

"You're wrong, After School Special. Totally wrong."

"And you're full of shit, Brooding Alpha Male." She folded her arms in front of her chest. "Why do you want back on the team?"

"Why do you think?"

"I have my theories, but I'd rather hear it from you."

"It's my job, Eva," he said plainly. "My paycheck. My family depends on me, and letting them down is not an option."

"Your... family?" Eva tried to swallow her shock. She'd always pictured him as an eternal bachelor who played hard and lived hard and had little time for anything else. It never occurred to her that he might be supporting other people.

Walker nodded, some of his hard edges softening as he continued. "Two brothers in college. My mom. She... Mom's in a long-term care facility. Alzheimer's. I mean, she's still okay—she lives in her own apartment there, takes pretty good care of herself. Wanders at night,

though. Gets confused. The docs thought it'd be best..."
Walker trailed off.

Oh, no. Eva didn't say anything. She couldn't. Sorry was such a tiny, pointless thing—a throwaway word that could never encapsulate all the things she was feeling for him in that moment. So instead, she stayed silent and placed her hand on his knee, hoping it was enough.

This time, he did jump at her touch, but he didn't pull away. To her surprise, he laughed.

"Oh, Mom would like you," he said. "Always says I need a strong woman to straighten my ass out. Take up where she left off."

"I think she did a pretty good job all on her own."

Walker turned to look at her, the emotion in his eyes unreadable. He wasn't shutting her out, exactly... more like weighing his options, trying to decide how much more he should say.

Eva understood. She was playing her cards close to the vest, too. Sharing too much, letting people in... it left you vulnerable. It was like giving someone the keys to your home, then leaving town for a year. You never knew when they might show up, let themselves in, and set the whole place on fire.

"I get it," she said now. "You want to take care of your family, and hockey is the best way you know how."

"It's the *only* way, Eva. Mom can't work. The boys

need to finish their education—that's non-negotiable. My old man split years ago—we didn't even hear that he died until six months after they'd buried his sorry ass. I'm all they've got. And pro hockey? That is damn lucrative."

Eva nodded. Walker was a talented player—nothing wrong with getting paid for that talent. But it wasn't enough to keep him motivated. Not when he was looking at months of grueling work just to get back on the team—and there were no guarantees of that happening, anyway.

Committing to this had nothing to do with money. It had everything to do with passion.

If Walker's heart wasn't in this, if his blood didn't run with the Tempest blue-and-silver, if his heart didn't beat to the sound of skates pounding down the ice, then there wasn't much more she or anyone else could do to get him through this recovery.

"Walker, I need to ask you this, and I need you to be completely straight with me. You mentioned your family, your job. But... do you even *like* hockey?"

He didn't respond right away, and for a moment she wondered whether he'd even heard her. But then he swung his leg over the bench, straddling it so their knees touched. He leaned forward, so close she could see the flecks of blue in his gray eyes, the tiny scar along his jawline, just under the dark stubble.

The sound of her heartbeat thudded loudly in her ears.

"First word," he said. "Hockey. Nine months old."

Eva laughed. "Please."

"Swear to God," he said.

"Sounds like something you tell the ESPN guys to make you more likable for the folks back home."

"Well, yeah, but it's also the truth." Walker laughed softly, his voice warm and intimate in the cavernous arena. "Before my dad split, he used to watch the games, chant at the TV." Walker pumped his fist. "Hock-ey, hock-ey, hock-ey. I picked it up from him, just started mimicking him one day. Couple years later, I inherited a pair of hand-me-down skates from my cousin. I was hooked. Mom started taking me to the rink at Delaware Park every weekend—she swears I skated better than I walked, despite my name." Walker shook his head. "I miss those days sometimes, sure. But I never stopped loving hockey. Never stopped wanting to play."

Eva smiled, finally seeing the light in his eyes, the joy, and she got it. Instantly. It wasn't that hard for her to remember feeling the same way about figure skating—like it was all she wanted, all she needed to live, no matter what else was going on around her.

This was the Walker Dunn she was looking for. The one she wanted to help. The one she truly believed she *could* help. The injury may have distracted him from his passion for a while, but deep down, it was still there. Still burning.

For the first time since their initial meeting, Eva *truly* wanted to help him—not for the money or the promise of a full-time job. She wanted to see him get back on the active roster. To succeed at the thing he obviously loved more than anything. To remember why he was doing this, why—family or not—he couldn't just walk away.

"I used to skate at Delaware Park, too, you know," she said. "With my dad. Mom always hated when I spent time alone with him—thought we were talking behind her back. But Dad didn't care. Every Saturday, crack of dawn, wind chill be damned, we were out on that ice. Mom was the last thing on our minds. For me, it was all about the ice, the cold air on my cheeks, the wind in my hair when I had a good run on that long straightaway."

"No shit? You were a fierce, badass little kid, weren't you?"

"Dad always said I had a strong competitive spirit."

"Yeah, well. If we ever crossed paths at the park, I'm sure you knocked me on my ass a few times."

"Obviously."

Walker grinned, lighting up the whole arena. Slapping his thighs, he said, "Guess it was fate that we ended up here together."

A white-hot spark zinged through her belly. Walker held her gaze, almost as if he was daring her to make a move. To lean in. To give him some indication that the insane heat rising between them was real—that it had been there from the first moment they met, and was still raging on, no matter how professional she tried to keep it, no matter how hard they pushed each other's buttons.

God, it would be so easy. Just lean in. Pick up where we left off the other day.

But she couldn't give that to him. Couldn't let him into her home like that. Into her heart.

Breaking their intense gaze, she forced a laugh. "You mean here on the ice, with me kicking your ass and you trying desperately to pretend you've got the upper hand?"

"Oh, you wish!" Walker nudged her with his knee, drawing her attention back to him. When she finally looked up at him again, his teasing smile was gone, replaced by a wolf's grin, the dark desire in his eyes clear. "I meant *here*, Evangeline. On this bench. About ten seconds from—"

"Crazy, right?" Eva plastered on a smile and pulled back, desperate to put some distance between them, to get them back on course. She had to. Everything he said, everything about him—the deep voice, the dark pools of his eyes, his scent—she was wet and wound up and about half a heartbeat from giving in...

No. It was just too scary to consider. She backed up a little more on the bench.

Ignoring the flash of disappointment in Walker's eyes, Eva nodded toward the rink. "Ready for another go, or do you need to rest the knee?"

His walls were back up in an instant, shutting her out in the cold once again. She knew she was probably giving him mixed signals, making it harder than it needed to be. But God. Every time they made a shred of progress, something happened to shut him down again. To freeze her out.

"Knee's fine, princess."

"Are you sure? We can rest for—"

"Repeating the same damn question doesn't change the answer." Walker stood up hard and fast—too fast. He lost his balance, his bad knee taking most of the weight to compensate. He winced, unable to hide it.

He dropped back onto the bench like a ton of bricks, the wood groaning in protest. Without a word, he unlaced his skates and slipped them off.

Eva sighed. She hated seeing him like this, frustrated and in pain. There was no easy way to say what she had to say next, so she took a deep breath and dove right in. "Walker, our sessions... this is just to help you skate better, to be fast enough to get you back into the running."

"Tell me something I don't know."

"Even if they agree to put you back in the lineup, you're going to have to practice with the team for weeks before you get a shot on the ice again. And honestly, I don't think you're ready for that. Physically *or* mentally."

"If you've got a point, princess, I'd appreciate you getting there sooner rather than later. I've got shit to do tonight."

"See! That's it right there." Eva pointed at his chest, the tension escalating between them again. The light-hearted moments they'd shared earlier evaporated, all the typical arguments and frustrations rushing right back in to fill the space. "That's what I'm talking about. Your attitude sucks, Walker. You say you love this game, but—"

"Don't you question that. Not ever. Hockey is my life. My first, last, and *only* love. Got it?"

That comment shouldn't have stung, but it did. Still, Eva pressed on. "Do you love it enough to keep pushing? To show up early and work your ass off for me at every session? To work your ass off for your coaches, your teammates, your trainers, even with that excruciating pain? Because that's what it's going to take, Walker. Pushing yourself so hard that you might end up on crutches for the rest of your life, or worse. And that's only for a *shot* at getting back in the game—not a guarantee."

Eva lowered her eyes to his knee. Walker's hand was curled protectively over his kneecap. She wasn't sure he even realized it.

"I'm not in pain," he said.

"You're full of shit."

"You're nagging me."

"You're fighting me every step of the way."

"I'm just trying to make you happy."

"Happy? This has nothing to do with my happiness and everything to do with yours." She leaned forward and unlaced her skates, yanking them off her feet. "If you refuse to see that—"

"How can I be happy when you're barking at me every—"

"Hey!" Eva jabbed her finger into his chest. "That's completely not the point, and you're just… you're acting like a… you won't—"

"Won't *what*, princess?" Walker's eyes flared again with desire, and in a flash, he grabbed her hand, pressed it flat against his chest. Behind his jersey and the solid wall of muscle and bone, his heart banged wildly.

Eva wanted to melt, right there on the bench, right into a puddle of anger and lust and her soft pink fleece.

"You feel that?" he asked.

She nodded, mute, her own heart leaping into her throat. Walker's hand was warm and firm on top of hers, strong and immovable, and all she could think was… *don't let go. Don't let me pull away.*

"That's what you do to me, Eva. Every fucking time I see you."

"So?" She hated that her voice was so weak and watery, but she couldn't focus on anything but the drumbeat of his heart against her hand.

He leaned in close, his voice low and sexy. "So now you've got one chance, princess. One chance to tell me to back off."

Eva jutted out her chin, defiant till the end. "And if I don't?"

Walker's mouth curled into that wolf's grin again, his gray eyes darkening. In that low, maddening voice that made her thighs tremble, he said, "If you don't, I'm taking you. Right now. Right on this fucking bench."

Eva couldn't speak. She couldn't remember how. Her mind echoed with the words... *taking you... right now... this fucking bench...* and her insides throbbed with desire. She'd never been so turned on, never wanted it so badly in her entire life.

She licked her lips, waiting for her brain to come to its senses. To put her body on lockdown, stop letting her desires make decisions. But her brain was obviously out for the holidays, because without warning, Eva's lips curved into a hungry smile of her own, and her next words seem to come from someone else entirely.

"Come on, forty-six," she whispered, leaning backward on the bench. "Show me what you're made of."

CHAPTER ELEVEN

Walker didn't need to be told twice.

As soon as the words were out of Eva's sweet little mouth, Walker was on top of her, pinning her down beneath him, grateful for the arena's solid, wide benches. She closed her eyes and arched her hips, grinding against him, and the moment she whispered his name, he captured her mouth with a kiss.

Despite the fire in his belly, not to mention the raging hard-on, he forced himself to take it slow, brushing her lips with his, inhaling the warm vanilla scent of her skin. He didn't know if he'd ever get another chance to taste her. To feel her. He wanted it to last.

"Don't tease me," she whispered, moaning into his mouth, pulling him closer.

Fuck, he'd never wanted anyone so much. For a minute he thought about taking her back to his house, getting her into the steam room, or better yet, a proper bed—some place soft and warm where he could take his sweet time making her come.

But neither of them would last that long.

Walker nipped at her bottom lip, sucking it between his teeth, running his tongue along the soft flesh. Another sound escaped her mouth, somewhere between a sigh and a moan, and then she parted her lips to let him in fully, her tongue sliding out to meet his, velvety smooth.

The taste of that kiss, that mouth… God, she was so fucking sweet. So soft. Walker had spent the last week imagining this, his lips on hers, her hot breath on his face, but his fantasies hadn't even come close to the real thing.

He kissed her mouth, tasted every inch of it, then moved on to her chin, her jawline, his tongue swirling in the soft hollow of her throat as his hands worked to unzip her fleece, revealing a white thermal underneath. She wasn't wearing a bra—*thank you, Santa*—and her dark nipples stretched the thin fabric, just begging to be sucked.

Walker slid his hands under the hem of her shirt, her skin hot to the touch. She flinched at first, then giggled.

"Sorry," he said, pulling back.

"No!" She grabbed his hands, guided them back under her shirt. "I like cold hands. It just surprised me."

He kissed her again, his hands crawling along the silky smooth skin of her belly, her ribs, and—*Jesus fuck*—the curve of those perfect breasts. He couldn't take it anymore. He needed to suck her. Hard.

Lowering his mouth, he kissed her nipple through the fabric, then bit, teasing the stiff peak with his tongue as she moaned in absolute pleasure. He sucked it into his mouth, then reached for her waist, grateful there was no button or zipper to get in his way as he slipped a hand down the front of her pants, desperate to feel her soft, wet heat.

He swallowed hard, his balls aching. "You're not wearing panties."

"No."

"It's like you knew I was coming."

Eva laughed. "Not exactly. It's just easier without them when I skate."

Holy shit. Walker almost came right there. "You're telling me that every time you're out on that ice with me, you're commando?"

Her cheeks pinkened, but Eva nodded.

Walker tried to think of something funny to say, but he couldn't speak. He was too fucking turned on.

He skimmed through her soft mound of hair, sliding two fingers inside her, coating them in her wetness. With his thumb, he traced a slow circle over her clit.

Eva's eyes fluttered closed.

"You okay?" he asked.

"I… yes. More," she said, fisting the front of his jersey and pulling him close. "Harder, forty-six."

Fuck, when she called him that… It turned him on so damn much he could hardly stand it.

He pulled his fingers out slow, then slid back in, teasing her inch by agonizing inch. "Like this?"

She shook her head, her thighs trembling. She was already close—damn close—and he wanted her to fucking *feel* it. To scream his name and know that he was the one who'd sent her over the edge.

"Tell me what you want, princess," he teased, sucking her nipple into his mouth again. The shirt was cold and damp from where he'd already licked her, and her nipple hardened to a diamond point at his renewed attention.

God, what I'd do to her if we were naked…

"Please," she panted. "I can't… I… Oh God, please. Harder."

She was right there—he could feel her tightening as he slid in deeper, fucking her breathless with his fingers. But it wasn't enough. Not for him. He wanted more of her. All of her.

"Take off your pants," he commanded. The air was cold, but neither of them seemed bothered by it, the heat between them chasing away the chill.

Eva shimmied out of the spandex and kicked them to the floor. "Tell me you have a—"

"Hang on." Walker slid off the bench and crouched down to reach his gear bag underneath, praying to God he still had some condoms in there from the team's last away game.

Come on, come on... bingo. His fingers closed around the strip like he was in the damn Hunger Games and just found the last scrap of food in the Cornucopia.

God, he couldn't wait to be inside her. To feel that gorgeous pussy clench around him as he brought her right over the edge.

Walker rose from the floor and yanked down his pants and thermals, freeing his aching cock from its confines.

And then he froze.

In his rush to get back to Eva, he'd forgotten about his scars. About the fact that outside of the medical profession, no woman had ever seen them. Not these.

Until now.

Eva's eyes widened, her mouth open in shock.

Walker got it. Some scars were sexy as hell. He had one hidden along his jawline, a few on his hands, a rather nasty one on his forearm—all of them badges of honor he'd earned on the ice that had made him feel tough, accomplished. And all of them had, at one time or another, driven the women in his life wild.

But the gash that ran down the front of his leg from pelvis to knee wasn't sexy. The one slashed across his inner thigh wasn't sexy. And neither was the one that snaked around his calf. They were angry and purple and jagged, constant reminders of the steel-and-glass monster that had nearly claimed his life.

Mostly, Walker tried not to look at his leg. If he looked for too long, all the old ghosts would rush him, the constant whiff of death still close at his heels.

It'd been six months, and every time he saw those damn scars, he felt like he'd gotten away with something he really, truly shouldn't have.

Wordlessly Eva reached forward, trailing her fingers along the ridges of the longest scar, the one that ran down the center of his leg. He flinched at first, then relaxed, her gentle caress sending tingles all the way up to his scalp. He hadn't been touched there—not like that —and the sensation of her soft fingers on the rough, puckered skin drove him wild.

She slid off the bench and onto her knees, urging him to sit down in front of her as she tugged his pants all the way off.

With a warm, delicate touch, Eva ran her hands up both of his calves, over his knees, up along the tops of his thighs. She glanced up at him through thick, feathery lashes, and in her amber eyes Walker saw no pity. Only the same fierce confidence she'd demonstrated on the ice. The fire that always made him want to do better, *be* better. The passion she seemed to bring into everything she did, and now she was bringing it here, right to him.

He was hard again in an instant, and Eva reached up and grabbed him, fisting him, stroking him as she kissed the scar along his inner thigh, her lips and tongue and breath blazing a hot path over his flesh.

Walker threaded his fingers into her hair, tugging it loose from that tight little bun. It was longer than he'd thought, spilling down through his fingers in waves that reached the middle of her back. He brushed his thumb across her lips, then urged her upward, pulling her onto his lap and guiding her legs around his waist.

"Is this... is your knee okay like this?" she asked.

He slid his hands around the bare curves of her ass as his cock brushed against her wet heat. "More than okay."

Walker tore open the condom and rolled it down on his shaft, then Eva shifted forward, tightening her thighs around his hips as she guided him inside, all the way to the fucking hilt.

Eva whispered his name, gripping his shoulders for balance as she rode him, slowly at first, then faster, harder, deeper as they found their perfect rhythm.

Everything about her was red-hot and explosive, her body stretching to accommodate him, then tightening around him, driving him out of his fucking mind.

He slid his hands up the back of her shirt, threading his fingers into the hair at the nape of her neck and pulling her in for a kiss as he arched his hips to meet her, thrusting deep, deeper still, Eva's fingers digging into his shoulders, her vanilla scent enveloping him fully. She was so tight, so slippery, so perfect... Walker couldn't handle all the sensations of Eva—her scent, the satiny feel of her skin, the soft sounds of her breath, the silky touch of that flame-red hair, the taste of her mouth— God, there was just so much, all at once. It made his head fucking spin.

Eva broke their kiss, pulling back to look into his eyes, her own gaze dark with pleasure. "You feel so amazing. Don't stop. Please don't stop."

She didn't look away, even as she said the words, even as she moaned for him, writhing against him, stroking him harder and faster. He couldn't look away; she had him locked in her blissed out gaze, totally spellbound by her unwavering confidence.

God, he fucking loved that about her.

"I'm close," she whispered.

Thank God. Walker didn't think he could last much longer, either. Not with her looking at him like that.

"Let go, princess," he whispered into her mouth, his tongue brushing her lips. "We're all alone here. Just us. Come for me."

"God, I'm... yes... Walker!" Eva gasped once more, then shattered, her fingers fisting his jersey as the orgasm tore through her body, everything inside her pulsating and hot as she rode him harder and harder, all the way to the blissful end, never once breaking their intense gaze.

Walker stared into the golden depths of her eyes as he felt his own white-hot orgasm build, build, build, his balls tightening, his muscles clenching tight, tighter, and *holy shit* he fucking exploded, so hard, so hot, emptying himself fully with a final shuddering thrust between her perfect, creamy thighs until he was utterly, completely spent.

With a contented sigh, Eva melted in his arms, resting her head against his chest as they sat in silence, slowly coming back to earth. Walker pressed his lips to the top of her head, counting the strong beats of his heart, and damn if he didn't want to stay on that bench with her forever.

But it was only a few minutes when he felt her shifting, the moment sliding away from them.

Slowly she untangled herself, rising off the bench and looking at him once more. Her smile was tentative, her skin flush with pleasure. He waited for her to say something, but she didn't, and he was too far gone for words.

They hunted for their pants and dressed in silence, and Walker sat on the bench and watched as Eva tugged the fleece down over her hips, then attempted to smooth her hair back into the bun. Her cheeks were pink, her lips puffy.

Walker was in a daze. He could still taste her, still feel

her electric touch. He didn't want to be done. Didn't want to go back out on the ice, back to the place where they fought and he ached and his whole career stood on the brink.

Because here, for just a little while, Eva Bradshaw had done better than go back in time.

She'd stopped it altogether.

CHAPTER TWELVE

"You're awful quiet," Roscoe said. "Things go okay with your ice skater today?"

Ignoring him, Walker reached forward and cranked up the heat, blasting the cabin of his truck. They were en route to Wellshire Place with a Christmas tree the size of Nebraska strapped to the roof, Roscoe's arm stretched out through the passenger window to keep it steady while Walker navigated a full-on lake effect snowstorm.

His mother had always loved Christmas—down-sizing from the house Walker had initially set her up in to the small assisted living apartment she now occupied at Wellshire had done nothing to alter her holiday deco-rating plans.

Nor had the impending blizzard.

"Well?" Roscoe pressed.

"Keep your hand on that tree and let me focus on the

road. I'm trying to avoid getting us killed, if that's cool with you."

Roscoe laughed. "So. You and the princess finally f—"

"The next words out of your mouth better be 'figured out that backward crossover move,' or I'll pull this truck over right now and leave your ass on the side of the highway."

"And disappoint the lovely ladies of Wellshire? I don't think so."

"My mother would support me on this."

"No way. Karen loves me."

Walker cracked a smile. It was true; his mother had fallen in love with Roscoe the first time she'd met him, years ago at one of the games, and Roscoe had been part of the family ever since. Yeah, she liked Henny, too, but he wasn't around as much—spent all his free time chasing women. Not like Roscoe. Walker loved both of those rat bastards equally, but of the two, Roscoe had always been more like a brother than a friend.

"You're right," Walker finally admitted, still keeping his gaze locked on the road. Visibility was shit, and cars were fishtailing up ahead. "We hooked up." Roscoe didn't need any more details. "And then she split. End of story."

"What? Why? What did you do?"

"Far as I can tell, nothing. She just… she said she had to go. Her ride was there."

"What about the rest of your sessions?"

Walker shrugged. "We're still meeting Monday morning, right on schedule, far as I know."

Roscoe didn't say anything, but Walker could tell he wanted to. Dude was about to explode.

"Just say it, asshole," Walker said.

"Dude. You can't fuck this up."

"I know."

"You need this. We all need it."

"I *know*."

"More than you need a roll in the sack. I'm serious, Walker."

Walker's hackles rose, but he let the comment pass. He knew Roscoe wasn't trying to insult his woman. He was just telling the truth—Walker *did* need this, and anything that interfered with his ability to get back in shape and back on the team was bad news.

The fact that he was already thinking of Eva as his woman was all the warning he should've needed.

Of course, Walker had never paid much attention to warning signs.

"Are you making *any* progress on your times?" Roscoe asked. "Or are you too busy putting the moves on the coach?"

"Christ, Roscoe. It's not like that. It just sort of… happened."

"Let me guess. You slipped on the ice, and fell on top of her, and—"

"Something like that, yeah." They'd finally arrived at Wellshire, and Walker slowly pulled up to the front, flicking on the hazard lights so they could unload the tree. He was grateful for the distraction—he was done justifying himself. "Listen, Roscoe. I appreciate the concern. But I'm handling this."

"You're handling *something*, all right."

"It won't happen again. Just a onetime thing."

"Whatever you say."

Walker could tell the man didn't believe him. Couldn't blame him, though. As usual, Roscoe could read him like a fucking book.

And as much as Walker wanted to believe that his time with Eva on that bench was a one-and-done thing, he couldn't. He didn't even know when it'd happened— the instant their lips touched? The instant he slid inside her? The instant she'd moaned his name and shuddered against him?—but Eva had lodged herself quite snugly into his mind, and no amount of logic or reason would get her out. He wanted to kiss her again. To feel her. To make her scream his name. To fall into the depths of her amber eyes, coming inside her as she trembled all around him…

"You with me, there, forty-six?" Roscoe smacked him in the chest, then cracked up, shaking his head as he climbed out of the truck.

"Right behind you, dickhole. Thanks."

The Wellshire was set up like a high-end condominium, with three floors of apartments that ranged in size from studios to three-bedroom suites. Most of the larger units were occupied by couples, but Walker's mother had a nice two-bedroom on the second floor with a view that looked out toward downtown Buffalo. She'd always loved the lights of the skyline, especially when they lit up City Hall in red and green for Christmas.

After shaking off the snowy bows outside, followed by some fierce negotiating with the elevator, Walker and Roscoe managed to get the tree up to his mother's apartment. Her door was already open, and a handful of folks were hanging out inside, gorging themselves on eggnog and Christmas cookies. Walker and Roscoe walked in to a warm chorus of cheers and laughter.

Walker smiled. The old ladies sure loved their hockey boys.

Inside, he handed off the tree to Roscoe, then gave his mom a quick kiss before heading out to move the truck. The snow was really coming down now—in the short time he'd been in the building, his truck had been covered in a thick, white blanket.

He managed to get the truck into a parking spot, but

the lot was an ice rink, and Walker didn't think it'd be long before they shut down the roadways.

Back inside, Roscoe had already gotten the tree into the stand in front of the big windows. Now he was holding court in the living room, Mom and her friends hanging on every word.

"I think it's good for him," Roscoe was saying.

"Walker," his mother said, waving him in from the doorway. "You get in here this minute." Her eyes sparkled, her tone both excited and admonishing, and Walker grinned, wondering how he could've gotten in trouble so quickly. "You didn't tell me you were working with Evangeline Bradshaw!"

Oh, shit.

He cut a mean glare to Roscoe. "Must've slipped my mind, but I see my friend filled you in."

His mother beamed. "Walker, that's incredible! Do you know how lucky you are to be working with her?"

"You *know* her?" Walker asked.

"Everyone knows Eva. She took home the silver in ladies figure skating on her first time at the Olympics— fifteen years old. A few years later, she won the gold."

"Everyone knew she would," one of his mom's friends chimed in.

His mother nodded sagely. "She also won four World Championships and five or six U.S. Figure Skating Gold

Medals. I used to save the Buffalo News articles about her."

Walker didn't know whether to be more impressed by the fact that Eva had kicked so much ass, or the fact that his mother seemed to know her on such an encyclopedic level.

It always amazed him how his mother could remember details like that from so many years ago, but not what she had for breakfast or what day of the week it was. The doctors kept warning him it would only get worse, too. Today was apparently a good day.

He wondered what Eva would say if she were standing here now, whether she'd be embarrassed or proud, whether she'd tell them stories from her days as a competitor, whether she'd shrug it off as if it were all part of the job. The only thing he knew for sure was that his mother—and her friends—would be absolutely charmed by her.

Just as Walker was.

Abruptly, he dismissed the thought, forcing Eva out of his mind. She would never be here, never meet his mom, never hang out with him socially. They had a professional arrangement, and that was it. Today had been a fluke, and the sooner he got that through his thick head, the better off they'd both be.

"The team set me up with her to work on my skating," he said firmly, kicking off his boots. "Short-term thing."

Mom waved away his words as if he were just being modest. "She's very pretty, Walker. I always loved that red hair of hers."

Don't remind me.

"You should bring her flowers," Lorraine, his mother's closest friend at Wellshire, offered. "Girls love flowers."

For fuck's sake.

"She's not a girl," Walker said. "She's my skating coach."

"And that's all she'll ever be if you don't make your move," Lorraine said.

Walker shoved a hand through his hair, eyeing the bottle of spiced rum on the kitchen table.

"I'm not making any moves," Walker said. "I'm perfectly happy being single. End of story."

"It's not natural, Walker." Lorraine clucked her tongue. "A good-looking young man like yourself, still single? We all know what that means." Her eyes trailed down to his—*Jesus.*

"I don't have any issues there, Lorraine. Thanks for your concern." Turning to Roscoe, he said, "This is all your fault."

"You know they make pills for that now?" Another woman—Paulette, the next-door neighbor who was always eating his mother's Lean Cuisines—added. "I probably have some samples at my place if you want to come check."

Roscoe busted up laughing. "Yeah, Walker. Maybe you should go check."

"Maybe I should beat your ass."

"Walker!" His mother narrowed her eyes. "Don't you talk to Roscoe like that. He's a good boy."

"He always talks to me like that, Karen," Roscoe pouted. "He's mean."

Walker chucked his wet gloves at Roscoe. "Get off your ass and help me get the lights on this tree before I string you up instead."

Roscoe laughed. "See what I mean? Such a brute."

While his mother and her friends refilled their eggnog cups, Walker and Roscoe untangled the lights from their epic knot, and got the entire tree lit to Mom's specifications, with alternating strands of solid and twinkling white lights.

"It looks like Rockefeller Center in here," Paulette said, beaming. She rose out of her chair, smoothing out her hair, which was a pretty damn close match to her light blue tracksuit. "Walker, come here by the tree. Take a selfie with me."

Walker obliged, putting his arm around her while she snapped a picture with her phone.

"One more," she said, squeezing in closer. Her arm

snaked around his waist, and then the crazy broad grabbed his ass.

"Okay, great, thank you, Paulette." He pulled out of her embrace and sat down on the couch next to his mother. Despite the heckling—not to mention the groping—he was thrilled to see his mother so happy, so lucid. He was even glad to have Roscoe here, spreading the holiday cheer.

He was still going to kick his ass later for telling them about Eva, but Walker was grateful that he'd come along.

"Walker," his mother said, "why didn't you bring Eva with you?"

"Ma, I told you. She's not my girlfriend. Just my coach."

"She doesn't like you?"

"Yeah, Walker," Roscoe said, nearly choking on his own laughter. "Doesn't she like you?"

Walker forced his jaw to unclench. "Not like that, no."

"Just ask her out," his mom said. "Don't make such a big deal about it. Invite her to dinner like a gentleman." She shook her head, rolling her eyes. "You kids today overcomplicate everything. All your matches and tinders and sexting—"

"Mom!"

"What? Sometimes you just have to show a girl you like her, and the rest happens on its own time."

"It'll happen a lot faster if you take the pill," Paulette added with a wink. "It'll last longer, too."

"On that note…" Walker shook his head, leaning over to kiss his mom's cheek. "We'd better get going before we get stuck here. I'll be back for dinner on Sunday."

"You aren't going anywhere," she said. "They've already closed I-90 in both directions."

"It's true." Pearl and Cora, two of the neighbors from across the hall, walked in, setting a fondue pot and bowl of bread cubes on the dining table, because apparently it was still 1974. "And they're expecting another five to six feet over the weekend. But don't worry. We've got plenty of food and booze."

Everyone cracked up at that. Saucy old broads.

Walker sank back into the couch. Buffalo blizzards were no joke. He was hoping he and Roscoe would be in and out tonight before the real bad stuff hit, but they'd missed their window.

He nodded at Roscoe. "Looks like we're in it for the long haul."

"Slumber party! Excellent!" Roscoe clapped once, his face lighting up with genuine excitement. "Who wants to play some pinochle?"

"I think we should sing carols," Lorraine suggested.

"You can stay in my suite, Walker," Paulette said, squeezing in on the couch on his other side and wrapping her hands around his bicep. "I've got *plenty* of room."

As Paulette crept closer, Lorraine and Roscoe led the rest of the neighbors in a rousing round of "Deck the Halls." His mother sang louder than all of them, nudging Walker in the ribs to get him to join in.

Walker didn't sing. Period.

Paulette had just gotten another handful of his ass when his phone finally buzzed with a text. Walker tried not to sigh audibly with relief.

"Sorry," he said, "I've got to take this."

He slid the phone from his pocket and looked at the screen, then excused himself to the kitchen, where he could smile like an idiot in private.

Eva.

CHAPTER THIRTEEN

"If you keep eating the popcorn, there won't be any left for the tree." Marybeth brushed a pile of kernels off of Gracie's lap, laughing as Bilbo Baggins rushed over to suck them up. "See, Eva? You don't have to worry about mice. Bilbo's on the job."

Eva laughed, but only because Gracie and Marybeth were doing it. She hadn't really been listening—couldn't even recall what Marybeth had said. Something about the dog?

"How's that garland coming, space cadet?" Marybeth nodded at the popcorn bowl in Eva's lap, still full.

"Huh?" Eva looked down at her hands. After twenty minutes with the thread and needle, she'd only gotten as far as stringing her first kernel.

"You've been on another planet since we picked you

up," Marybeth said. Then, under her breath, "Must've been *some* practice."

Marybeth was right. Eva didn't even remember the ride home. She'd left Walker sitting on the bench, her mind in a fog as she made her excuses—ride waiting in the parking lot, storm coming in—and bolted out of there, certain that if she spent another minute in his presence, she might just come undone. Now she was hanging out in her living room with her family, toasty and warm by the crackling fire, Mariah Carey singing her Christmas heart out through the speakers, her sense of time gone.

Eva blinked, her eyes drifting to the big window behind the tree. Just beyond the reflection of the tree's twinkling colored lights, snow swirled in the glow of the street lamps outside, thick and furious.

"I... what time is it?" she asked. *How is it already dark outside? Didn't we just get home?*

"Almost seven. You hungry?" Marybeth rose from the couch, dusting the renegade popcorn kernels off her hands. "I should probably check on the lasagna."

"Lasagna?" Eva blinked again, the snow outside blurring into the darkness as the smell of tomato sauce and garlic finally registered. She'd totally forgotten about dinner—they'd put it in the oven an hour ago. "Oh, shoot! I'll do it—you guys keep working on the garlands."

"There's salad in the fridge," Marybeth said. "Take the Italian dressing out for me?"

In the tiny kitchen, Eva slid the lasagna out of the oven and popped in the garlic bread, trying her damnedest to stay in the moment. It was a perfect night —trimming the tree with her daughter and sister, Christmas songs drifting through the house, lasagna cooling on the rack. Eva loved getting snowed in like this, totally cozy while the storm raged outside. Marybeth was spending the night, so once Gracie went to bed, the sisters would stay up until the wee hours talking, drinking wine, and getting a head start on the Christmas cookies. These were the moments she loved most about the holidays.

But for some reason, she couldn't get her mind off Walker.

"Some" reason. Oh yes, it's a real mystery!

Eva checked her phone, but there were no missed calls or texts. She tried not to be disappointed.

Eva wasn't particularly experienced when it came to men, but it's not like she'd never hooked up before. Gracie was proof of that. Still, being with Walker had been unlike anything she'd ever experienced—anything she'd ever even imagined. His touch was so hot, so electric. She was still reeling from his every kiss, his words, the gravel edge of his voice. And the way he'd made her feel... she'd never before felt so certain, so confident about her body and what she needed, about how good it felt to be touched, to be held. Walker had not only given her that pleasure, but had made her feel—without so much as a word—that she deserved it. That she should embrace it. When they'd locked eyes... damn. She didn't know him well—not really. But in that moment, they'd shared something so intimate, so rare.

All she could think about now was whether she'd ever have a chance to look into those eyes like that again.

The thought made her knees weak, her insides burn in the best possible way.

God, the things he'd said to her... the way he'd taken control, thrusting so perfectly inside her as she wrapped her legs around his waist and rode him, hard and fast, their bodies matched as if they'd been made for each other...

Pull yourself together, woman!

Eva took the salad out of the fridge, then stared at the bottles of salad dressing on the door rack, trying to remember which one Marybeth had asked for. Ranch? French? It was pointless. Her thoughts were consumed with Walker. With the things they'd said and done. With the fact that he hadn't called.

You are so sentimental and crazy.

It's not like they'd made any promises. It was just a onetime thing, and anyway, she's the one who'd bolted out of there like a scared little mouse.

Eva chewed on her thumbnail, her gaze flicking between the blank phone screen and the blustery snow swirling outside the kitchen windows.

You're being ridiculous. Just send him a text!

Relenting, she pulled up his name in the contact list.

Hey, it's Eva, she texted. *Roads look pretty bad... just checking that you got home okay.*

His reply was immediate, sending a little zing through her stomach. *Miss me already, princess?*

Ha! Just protecting my meal ticket! You staying warm?

Your concern is touching. Pretty sure I won't be cooling down any time soon—your fault.

Heat crept up Eva's neck. She knew the feeling.

Are you home? she asked, wondering for the first time where he lived. What his house looked like. Whether his bedroom smelled like him.

At Mom's place w/ Roscoe to put up her tree, now crashing here till the roads clear. Mom & her friends insisted. They're all here singing Christmas carols & causing a damn ruckus.

Eva smiled, picturing the scene. Old folks, twinkling white lights, lots of laughter. They probably loved Walker and Roscoe.

Aww, that's sweet, she texted. *Sounds cozy.*

Cozy? Have you ever spent the night with a bunch of old women drunk on spiked eggnog?

No, but that's definitely going on my bucket list now.

When they're not singing, they're giving me sex advice, Eva. There's not enough rum in this eggnog.

Haha... take good notes!

Are you saying I need pointers? Walker asked. *I don't recall any complaints earlier. Or were you screaming my name for some other reason?*

Eva nearly melted at his words. Her mouth was watering for his kiss, for his touch, everything inside her going fizzy at the memories. *I think you know the reason, 46.*

Hmmm. Where are you right now?

Home. Kitchen. Getting dinner ready.

Are you still pantyless? he asked.

Ah, yes. Pantyless skating coach by day, pantyless chef by night. It's my superpower.

Don't suppose you want to come save me?

What about the roads?

You can sleep over.

Eva laughed out loud. *At your mom's place? Will we have to sleep in separate rooms?*

Yeah, but we could sneak down to the rec room after the oldies go to bed.

You are definitely going on the naughty list, 46!

I'll save you a seat, he texted. *A BENCH seat. I hear you like those.*

!!! You are—

A sudden, piercing wail tore through the house,

cutting Eva off mid-text. Only then did she look up and notice the gray haze filling the kitchen.

"Eva! What are you doing?" Marybeth rushed past her, yanking open the oven door and flicking on the exhaust fan. Smoke poured from the oven, the blackened remnants of the garlic bread visible behind her.

"You could've burned the house down!" Marybeth said, cracking open the window over the sink. Snow blew in through the gap, swirling onto the countertops. The smoke detector continued its warble, Bilbo Baggins howling right along with it, running into the kitchen with Gracie on his heels.

Gracie mashed her hands over her ears. "What happened?"

"Your mother was texting when she should've been cooking," Marybeth said, shooting Eva a glare that meant they'd be discussing this later. Her sister was practically a mind reader; Eva was surprised she'd held out this long without bringing up Walker. Eva suspected she'd be getting an earful the moment Gracie was in bed later.

"It's fine," Eva said, grabbing a dishtowel and waving it around the room to dissipate the smoke. "Garlic bread is no longer on the menu, though."

"And it's snowing in our kitchen." Gracie pointed to the window, the curtains billowing out in the icy breeze as the smoke detector screamed and the dog cowered under the table. Eva, Marybeth, and Gracie burst out laughing.

As Eva climbed up on a step stool to reset the smoke detector in the archway, she looked down at her family crowded into the small yellow kitchen—her daughter, her sister, her sweet dog—and was overcome with a sense of love and gratitude so powerful, it brought tears to her eyes. No, her situation right now wasn't perfect, but she'd been so, so blessed in her life. Blessed with love and abundance, blessed with a passion for ice skating, blessed with opportunities to find meaningful work, and blessed especially with this family. Looking at them now, their big smiles, the music of their laughter a harmony to her own, Eva felt both hopeful and determined, buoyed by their unfettered joy to work hard to secure that job with Doug McKellen, to make life better for all of them.

The phone in her back pocket buzzed with a text, and her heart gave a little start, but she didn't dare check her messages.

She didn't quite know where Walker Dunn fit into the picture.

She just knew—in that moment, the realization coming so fast and furious it nearly knocked her off the stool—that he did.

CHAPTER FOURTEEN

After cleaning up the dinner dishes and getting the rest of the ornaments on the tree, Eva finally got Gracie settled into bed. She was uncorking a nice bottle of Merlot one of her students' moms had given her when Marybeth—nearly bursting at the seams—finally brought it up.

"Are you going to tell me what's going on," Marybeth asked, "or do I have to resort to blackmail?"

"*You* blackmail *me*?" Eva teased. "Not unless you want Nate to find out about your mime phase in college."

"Oh my God! Ben wasn't a mime! He was a street performer."

"I can't imagine what he was like in bed." Eva held out her hands, pushing against an invisible box that was getting smaller with each passing second.

Marybeth cracked up. "Don't quit your day job, sister. And quit stalling! Just tell me what's going on with the hockey man."

The hockey man.

Eva still hadn't been able to return his texts, and judging from the vibrating in her pocket, he'd sent a few more. The phone was practically burning a hole in her pants, but Eva kept her face neutral, her eyes focused on the task at hand.

She filled their wineglasses, then set the bottle on the coffee table and settled back on the couch next to Marybeth, clinking their glasses in cheers. "To mysteries."

"To sisters before misters," Marybeth amended.

"To one sister killing the other and making it look like an accident."

"To the dead sister rising up out of the grave and calling Mom to come over and help bake cookies."

Eva's eyes went wide. "You wouldn't!"

"Why test me? I'm unreliable when I drink." Marybeth chugged her wine, trying not to laugh and shoot it out her nose.

Eva sighed. *Might as well rip off the Band-Aid.* "We had sex."

Marybeth jumped up off the couch so fast, she nearly dropped her glass.

"Watch it!" Eva said, laughing. "That's expensive stuff!"

"I *knew* it! I knew you looked different after the practice. Your hair was a wreck, for one thing. And your lips were puffy. *And* you've been completely distracted ever since we picked you up. I can't believe you! I *so* called this one." Marybeth sat back on the couch, a self-satisfied grin stretching across her face. "That was him you were texting before, right?"

Eva rolled her eyes. "Nice detective work, Sherlock."

"So..." Marybeth tucked her feet up underneath her, covering her legs with the red fleece blanket from the back of the couch. "How was it?"

"Hot as hell, that's how." Eva's cheeks flamed. What had happened with Walker... damn. It'd felt intimate in a way that sex never had before, crazy as that sounded. It was intense, it was rare, and the details were something that Eva wanted to keep to herself.

She sipped some more wine and turned away.

For all Marybeth's teasing, she knew exactly when to push, and when to back off, and Eva was grateful for the momentary silence.

It was still snowing like crazy outside, and Eva's thoughts drifted again to Walker, wondering if he was having fun at his mom's place. She tried to picture him there with Roscoe, hanging out with his mother and her friends, but she didn't know what the woman looked like. Did Walker resemble his mother, or his father? Did she ever attend his hockey games? What were his brothers like?

The fact that Eva was pondering all of this should've been a red flag right there, but she couldn't help herself. She wanted to get to know him. To know about his family and the people who loved him. To know what his life was like off the rink.

She sipped her wine, her gaze wandering away from the window, landing on the stack of mail at the end of the coffee table. There were a few Christmas cards from neighbors and friends, but the rest of the envelopes were bills, including the year-end notice from the health insurance company about rate hikes. Her premium was going up by three hundred dollars a month next year.

More than ever, she needed that job with McKellen to come through. Getting involved with Walker put that job at risk, which was completely stupid and reckless.

And yet...

The fire popped and crackled before them, bringing Eva back to the moment. She stretched out her legs on the couch, her feet seeking Marybeth's under the blanket.

"Soooo," Marybeth said softly, her eyes dancing mischievously in the glow of the firelight, "do you like him? Or was this just a fling?"

"I barely know him, Marybeth. What do you think?"

"Oh, you totally like him. It's so obvious!"

"I..." Eva let the denial die on her lips. She *did* like

him. Which was not only bad for the job situation; it went against every one of her personal survival instincts. "It's a bad idea, right?"

Marybeth grabbed the bottle of wine and topped off her glass, then said, "I'm your sister and best friend. Do you need me to talk you out of this… or into it?"

"I need you to be honest with me. Am I nuts?"

"You tell me. I mean, you always said that hockey players were off limits. Like, no way, no how, nuh-uh, *seriously* off limits."

"They are. They *should* be." Eva shook her head, flustered at the tug-of-war raging in her heart. "There's just… there's something about him." She knew it sounded cliché and ridiculous, but that didn't make it any less true. "It's like we bicker constantly, pushing each other's buttons, and then he looks at me and smiles and…" Her skin heated at the memory, her thighs clenching, her mouth watering. "Marybeth, being with him…. Everything about it was absolutely incredible. Not just the physical stuff."

"So you guys connected," Marybeth said. "A spark. Maybe it's just really great chemistry."

Eva nodded. Yes, they'd had a connection. But it was more than a spark, more than a release of pent-up sexual tension. She and Walker had been amazing together, from the very first touch, the very first kiss.

From the first time she'd seen him on the ice, all

swagger and sex-on-skates, she'd felt it. That fire between them. The one that went beyond attraction, beyond chemistry. Beyond anything even remotely explainable.

It had felt familiar. Warm.

It had felt like coming home.

Which was precisely why she needed to shut it down.

They had a professional arrangement—one she couldn't risk losing. The notice from her insurance company drove that message home loud and clear. Like it or not, Eva needed that full-time job to come through more than she needed a man—even one as intriguing as Walker. Getting involved with him in any capacity off the ice—even just for one more sinful, delicious night— could put her entire future in jeopardy. What if things went bad between them? What if he decided to trash her reputation to his coaches and McKellen? One bad word from Walker, and she could kiss that job in Saint Paul goodbye.

And as much as Eva wanted to keep an open mind, to treat every person as an individual with no judgment, she couldn't help but be jaded by her past. The last and only other hockey player she'd ever gotten involved with had given her Gracie… and then he'd broken her. The painfully sharp contrast still threatened to tear her heart apart, and that pain was a near-daily reminder of how dangerous love could be.

That wasn't *love, and you know it…*

Eva closed her eyes. No, that man had never loved her, despite his promises. But he was the first and only man she'd ever opened up her heart to, and the agony he'd caused was more than she could ever bear again. Some days, she wondered how she'd survived at all. If not for Gracie, she honestly didn't think she would have.

As far as Eva was concerned, only a fool would set herself up for that kind of devastation again.

"Maybe you're right," Eva said. "I haven't been with a guy in so long, and Walker is so… hot," she trailed off, hating the lack of conviction in her voice.

"That look in your eyes is more than just infatuation with a hot guy."

Eva couldn't deny it.

"Did you tell him about Gracie?" Marybeth asked.

"What? No. Why would I? My personal life is none of his business."

"Eva. The man knows what you sound like when you—"

"Marybeth!"

"I'm just saying." Marybeth laughed. "That's pretty damn personal."

"It's not the same, and you know it." Gracie was Eva's. She wasn't about to share her with any old stranger, to expose her to anyone who could hurt her. Eva was having a hard enough time drawing her own boundaries with Walker—she didn't need to add Gracie to the mix. "Besides, just because we had sex doesn't mean I want him involved in my life. We work together. And today was just a onetime thing. It *has* to be. Because... reasons. End of story."

"I've read stories like that," Marybeth said. "They never end how you think they're going to."

"Well, this one will. It already has. I can't be with him again—not like that. It's totally unprofessional."

Marybeth considered this, then shrugged. "If you're that concerned about it interfering with work, can't you just hook up at the end? You've only got, what, five more weeks with him?"

Eva picked up a snow globe from the end table, giving it a good shake. It was one of her favorite Christmas decorations—a gift from her father when she was five, the first year she'd won a local competition. Inside, a tiny figure skater balanced on the ice before a swath of evergreens, all lit up for the holidays. The blue-and-silver snow fell down around her, catching in the trees, and Eva smiled, remembering how badly she'd wanted to live inside that snow globe when she was a kid. How badly she'd wanted a perfect fairytale life, suspended in time, where the snow never stopped falling, the ice never melted, and it was always Christmas.

"It's not just the sessions with Walker." Eva set down the snow globe and took a deep breath, steadying herself. She hadn't planned on telling Marybeth about the job offer—not until it was more certain—but she didn't want to keep it a secret any longer. Not from her sister. If it all worked out, Eva and Gracie would be moving out of state in a few months. She wanted Marybeth to know. She wanted them to spend as much time as possible together before everything changed.

And, Eva admitted to herself, she wanted Marybeth to be happy for her. Her sister's opinion meant more to Eva than anyone else's on the planet, and Marybeth would never lead Eva astray. If Marybeth thought it was a bad move, Eva wasn't going. It was that simple.

"There's something I haven't told you yet," Eva said.

Marybeth reached for the wine bottle. "Do I need more wine for this news?"

"Maybe?" Eva sighed. "There's actually a pretty big job offer on the line here." She told Marybeth about McKellen's offer, and Marybeth's whole face lit up with excitement. "The thing is," Eva said, "it's in Saint Paul."

"Minnesota?" Marybeth asked. Her mouth hung open in shock.

Eva let the silence drift between them again, giving Marybeth a moment to process. Of course Marybeth would want her to stay in Buffalo, but Marybeth wasn't their mother. She wouldn't manipulate Eva. Wouldn't lie to her about what was truly the best choice.

Eva topped off her own glass, then finally met her

sister's eyes again. "I never thought I'd leave New York, but I feel like I need a fresh start. I'm in a rut, Marybeth. The bills are piling up, the tuition thing is hanging over my head like a freaking cloud of darkness… I can't seem to get ahead here. This job… it's just about perfect for me. Well, other than the location."

"And the constant exposure to hockey boys," Marybeth teased lightly.

"At least they're nice to look at."

Marybeth smiled and held up her wineglass. "Tradeoffs."

After a beat, Eva reached forward, tucking a lock of hair behind Marybeth's ear. "You do so much for us. You have no idea what it means to me to have you in my life. Nate, too. I love you both so much. I just… I need this. I need to be able to support my family and not rely on favors."

"Okay, first of all, you're my sister. Gracie's my niece. It's not a favor—it's family." Marybeth glared at her, as if she were trying to brand the word right into Eva's heart.

But family wasn't just a word. Not to them. When their mother divorced their father when the girls were teenagers, and Mom became even more distant and cruel, Eva and Marybeth made a pact: from that moment on, they would choose their *own* family, blood or not. It was just a handy coincidence that they were related, they'd reasoned; they would've chosen each other anyway. Years later, Marybeth fell in love with and married Nate, and their family expanded. Gracie was born, and their family expanded again.

Their mother was part of their lives, but not part of their *family*. Neither of them wasted time with platitudes about how much their mother loved them deep down, or about how she only wanted what was best for them. The truth was, their mother was a very selfish woman, and both girls had spent their childhoods—and a good part of their adult lives—chasing affection that was always just out of reach, dangled before them only to be snatched away when they got too close.

The times over the years when they'd longed for a mother's affections, they vowed instead to be each other's mothers, offering the guidance, the friendship, and yes—even the tough love—that would otherwise go missing from their lives.

Eva and Marybeth took care of each other, not because they were obligated to, but because they wanted to. They'd chosen to, again and again.

"You leaving Buffalo doesn't change a thing, Eva," Marybeth said, her voice softer now, full of love and support. She reached under the blanket and squeezed Eva's foot. "Anyway, I'll be there as often as I can. In fact, I'm going to start planning my vacation time now so I can help you guys settle in."

"I don't even know if I'll get the job. It kind of depends on Walker."

"Nah. You'll get it. And you'll kick so much ass. I know it." Marybeth beamed, even as she wiped tears from her eyes. "God, Eva. I'm so proud of you. This job sounds perfect for you."

Eva blew out a pent-up breath, relief and love washing over her, her own eyes wet with tears.

"I'm happy for you," Marybeth said. "I'll miss you like hell, but I'm really, really happy for you." She held up her glass and touched it to Eva's, beaming. "To new adventures."

"And to family."

Marybeth smiled. "You are such a sap."

"I learned from the best."

The girls finished off the wine, then opened another bottle, talking and dreaming about the future, about possibilities, about hope.

When the fire had burned down to embers and the wine had finally run dry, Marybeth said, "Well, I guess there's not much point in getting attached to him, then."

"No," Eva agreed, as much as the thought made her feel hollow and sad. "And I'm definitely not getting attached—not to Walker or anyone else."

She was just enjoying a little harmless flirting—no strings. Besides, even if there *were* strings, how far could they really take this thing? If all went according to plan,

Eva would be leaving town in a few months, and Walker would be back on the active roster, traveling the country with his team, breaking records, his brief time with Eva on the ice a distant memory for both of them.

"I'm really not, Marybeth," she said again, but even in her severely buzzed state, she knew the words weren't true.

Not by a long shot.

CHAPTER FIFTEEN

Practice could not come soon enough.

Walker had spent the whole weekend texting with Eva, and the thought of seeing her again was the only thing that had gotten him through being stranded at Wellshire for three days. After that insane lake effect storm, when the sun finally rose Monday morning and Henny showed up to dig the truck out of the parking lot, Walker wanted to run into the street and kiss the rock-salted pavement.

But now that he was on the ice, geared up and ready to go, his insides were a tangled damn mess. The roads were fine, so why was she late? Eva was never late. Their texts had gotten pretty steamy last night—was she freaked out? Did he push her too far? Maybe she was regretting what'd happened Friday. What they'd done.

Or maybe you're acting like a fifteen-year-old boy who just got his first blowjob, asshole.

Walker checked his phone once more, then dropped it into his bag, doing another lap around the rink to work off some of his restless energy. On his third time around, she appeared, stepping out onto the ice in her skates, still trying to zip up her fleece.

"Sorry," she said, her cheeks pink. Her red hair was everywhere, falling down past her shoulders in damp waves. "I had to drop off... something. At my sister's place. Roads are still a little dodgy."

"I'm glad you're safe," he said.

"You, too." She finally smiled, and up came the damn sunshine. "I bet your mom was sad to see you go this morning."

"Not as sad as Paulette."

"I'll bet." Eva cracked up. Walker had told her the whole story over text, updating her with Paulette's antics all weekend. "You're such a heartbreaker, forty-six."

"What can I say? Ladies love me."

"Especially the blue-haired set."

"And the red." Walker reached forward, brushing the hair out of her face. He couldn't help it; his fingers ached to touch her.

Eva's breath caught, though Walker wasn't sure if it was his words or his touch that had given her a start.

"You're beautiful, princess," he said, trailing his

fingers across the silky-smooth skin of her cheek. She closed her eyes and leaned into his touch, taking a moment to catch her breath.

"Tell me what you're thinking about," he said.

"You," she whispered. It sounded like a confession, like she'd been caught doing something she shouldn't have been.

Despite Walker's best efforts to stay cool, his heart hammered in his throat. "Hmm. I guess I made quite an impression. And look, it's only Monday."

Eva laughed, but the joke made her open her eyes, made her pull back. Walker regretted it immediately.

"That's not what I mean." Her smile faded into a sigh, and Walker braced himself for the gut-punch of rejection. "Yeah, you made an impression. But we still have a job to do, forty-six. A big one."

Walker cracked a smile. "Trust me when I say I'm highly motivated to keep impressing you. With a big one."

"I'm serious!" She smacked him playfully on the chest, her eyes sparkling. "I need you at a hundred percent. Focused and ready to work harder than you've ever worked in your life."

He slid his arms around her waist and pulled her close, eliminating the space between them. God, they just fit together, their bodies lining up in all the right places, responding to each other almost instantly. He could feel it in the quickness of her breath, the beat of her heart, the tremble in her legs she was trying so hard to hide. And Walker? He was already hard, already imagining what it might be like to take her on that bench again. "I don't think *hard* is going to be a problem, princess."

"Walker..." Eva let out a moan as he pressed against her, but despite her soft smile, she placed her delicate hands on his chest and sighed. She wasn't pushing him away, exactly, but hell... she may as well have been. Every one of her signals was suddenly telling him to back the fuck off.

Saving her the trouble of asking, he stepped back, put some space between them.

Something like regret flashed in her eyes, but then it was gone. Her arms dropped to her sides, and just like that, Eva and Walker were back to business.

Nice job, dick. You totally freaked her out.

"The knee feeling okay?" she asked.

Walker's head was spinning. Fucking her was supposed to have eradicated her from his mind. Cleared out all the sexual tension and the naughty, curious thoughts so they could get back to work with nothing lingering between them. But now that he'd had a taste of her, and they'd spent the whole weekend teasing and flirting and all-but-sexting on the phone, all his hopes of getting back to normal were dashed. He was craving her, needing her, wanting her in a way he'd never felt about a woman in his whole damn life.

And he was fucking doomed.

She slicked her hair back, wrapping it into a bun with a rubber band she'd had around her wrist. "Ready to rock?"

He thought about making another joke, another innuendo, anything to see that light in her eyes again. But in the end, he only nodded, and Eva pressed her pretty lips together in a tight and completely professional smile, skated over to where she'd left her bag on the bench, and pulled out her clipboard and stopwatch.

CHAPTER SIXTEEN

Walker had barely touched her—just fingers on her cheek—and already Eva was ridiculously, embarrassingly wet.

Her mind was on autopilot as she guided him through the drills, recorded his times, shouted out pointers for better positioning and more speed and less energy expenditure and all the stuff she knew by heart, which was a good thing, because his touch had once again left her completely incapable of original thought.

She was pretty sure she wasn't fooling anyone with all that "let's get to work" stuff—especially not Walker. She made it through two more sets of slalom drills when she finally dropped her clipboard, skated straight for him, and slammed him against the boards.

Walker wasn't the type to wait for an invitation. One look into her fierce, desperate eyes, and he dropped his stick, slid his fingers into her hair, and lowered his mouth to hers in a white-hot kiss that made her toes curl up inside her skates.

McKellen's words echoed… *full-time… salary and benefits…* but the memory was fading fast, replaced instead by the sound of her own breath, her own heart-beat, the soft sighs escaping her mouth as Walker kissed her senseless.

There was no point in denying her desire, in pretending she didn't want Walker's hands on her bare skin, his mouth on her most sensitive places. She let him lead her off the ice, back toward the bench she now thought of as theirs, but that wasn't his final destination. The moment they'd stepped out of their skates, he grabbed her hand and led her further up the shallow concrete steps, all the way up to the viewing suite at the top.

The room was larger than it looked from the outside, with plush carpeting that smelled new and several leather chairs and couches. A mahogany bar set up with tall, leather-covered stools bisected the open front area, all of it offering a perfect view of the entire rink.

"Wow," she said, breathless and a bit dizzy. But Walker hadn't brought her here to admire the view. Before she could say another word, he kissed her again, deep and desperate, dropping to the floor and bringing Eva right down with him. They were on the floor, that thick, luxurious carpet soft on her back and shoulders as Walker kissed a searing hot path down the front of her thermal, tugging the pants down over her hips.

He pulled back, a slow, appreciative grin stretching across his face as he took in the view.

"Are those..." He leaned in close, inspecting the little red-and-green pattern on her white panties. "Mistletoe?"

Eva nodded, her cheeks flaming. Her sister had given them to her as a joke this weekend, and now she wondered whether wearing them had been a mistake. She'd hoped that adding an extra layer between her flesh and Walker's mouth would help her avoid giving in to the very desire coursing through her veins, but now she resented them. She wanted nothing more than for Walker to tear them off with his teeth and plunge his tongue deep inside her aching flesh.

"I thought you didn't wear panties on the ice." Walker's voice was gravelly, his eyes dark with desire.

"Not normally, no. But these... they're... festive." Eva smiled, the sound of her wild heart throbbing in her ears. "'Tis the season!"

"You're fucking adorable." He flashed that wolf's grin, then lowered his mouth to her thigh, kissing her with a powder-soft touch that left her trembling and begging for more. She arched her hips to get closer, but Walker was in complete control, teasing her with his lips, his tongue, whispering against her flesh about all the ways he wanted to make her come.

"I want to taste you," he said, licking the sensitive skin where the lace of her panties curved across her abdomen. He kissed her through the fabric, blowing a hot breath against her clit, then pulling back, inhaling her scent, his impossibly strong hands sliding the panties down off her hips, then slowly guiding her thighs apart.

Eva was out of her mind, writhing beneath him, slowly losing touch with reality. Her nerves were over-loaded with sensations—the tug and tangle of her hair rubbing against the carpet, the scent of Walker's skin close and warm, the hot press and release of his tongue as it circled her bellybutton, the taste of his name in her mouth as she let it fall softly from her lips.

She wanted more, all, rough, soft, hot, hard, slow, fast... Her thoughts were unspooling faster than she could pin them down. She slid her hand inside her own shirt, cupping her breast, pinching her nipple until it ached with delicious pleasure. Walker whispered her name against her thigh, and she threaded her fingers into his silky hair, twining deeper, urging him closer to her center, desperate to feel his hot, wet mouth against her flesh.

"You have no idea how bad I want you," he said, so close his lips brushed teasingly across her clit, the vibration of his deep voice rattling right down through her core. "Fucking hell, Eva."

She moaned in response. He pinned her thighs to the floor and slid his tongue inside her, stroking deeper, harder, then slow, his breath and lips teasing her clit as his tongue tasted every bit of her. She arched her hips and pulled him closer, warmth swirling in her belly, spreading on an electric current to her arms and legs, heat building between her thighs as Walker licked and sucked and teased, stroking her faster now, faster and harder and deeper as the lights blurred and her thighs shook and she fisted his hair and screamed his name as everything inside her exploded, all at once, hot and bright and beautiful.

It felt like days before Eva finally came back to her body, before she could finally remember how to make words. She propped herself up on her elbows and watched in awe as Walker kissed the curve of her knee, her thigh, her hipbone. When he finally got to her mouth, he hesitated, and she pulled him close, kissing him as deeply as he'd kissed her. His lips were warm and salty, the skin around his mouth damp with her arousal, and her heart hammered a new beat inside her chest.

He's mine, she thought.

And then she pulled back, a scared little mouse once again, tugging those silly Christmas panties back into place.

"I don't do this," she said breathlessly. "I mean, I *did* do it. But I really don't do it. This. Ever."

Walker laughed softly, and she forced herself to meet his eyes. He was smiling at her, his hair wild from her touch. "Princess. What are you even talking about?"

"This." She motioned between them, her hands like nervous little birds. "Hook up with... with clients. Why did you..." She closed her eyes, took a deep breath. Opened them again, but he was still watching her, amused. "Why did you even do that?"

"Do what?" he teased. "Kiss you so hard I made you come?"

"Kiss me *there*. Like... that. The way you.... God!" Words were escaping her again, the ache between her thighs too fresh, too sweet. Her body was still calling to his, missing the weight of him.

Walker grinned and cocked his head, clearly enjoying this particular bit of torture. "You're wearing mistletoe panties, princess. Where was I *supposed* to kiss you?"

"You *weren't* supposed to kiss me. That's the whole point. Just... clients and coaches shouldn't hook up."

"That's not what you said Friday. Or all weekend. Or down on the ice when you practically jumped me against the boards."

"What? I did no such thing."

Walker wagged a finger at her. "Santa doesn't like

liars, Evangeline. They go straight on the naughty list with all the other bad girls."

Eva swallowed. She knew she was being crazy. What the hell was wrong with her? They obviously liked each other. Why couldn't they just have a little fun? See where things went?

Because you are already getting way too attached. And in three months, you need to be gone.

"It's just... it's inappropriate," she said weakly. Walker's smile finally faded. Eva didn't know whether to be relieved or disappointed.

"You are the *queen* of mixed signals," he said, blowing out a breath. "But you're lucky. Because in addition to being a hockey god, I'm also a genius."

Eva couldn't help but smile. God, he was infuriating.

"Is that so?" she said.

"Bet your mistletoe-covered ass it is. And I've got a solution to this whole situation."

She rolled her eyes playfully. "I can't *wait* to hear this."

"I'm taking you to dinner tonight."

"What?"

"Six p.m. Text me your address, and then go home and put on something nice." His eyes trailed down her body, lingering on her thighs. "Or festive."

Eva's head was spinning again, a side effect she was

quickly getting used to with Walker. "Dinner? That's your genius solution?"

He met her eyes, the fire in his gaze filling her belly with butterflies. "I'm taking you on a date, Eva. Then I won't be just a client, and you can get over your little hang-up."

Eva pressed her lips together, considering. It was a bad idea, but… "Fine. But it's not a date. It's a work meeting. Team-building exercise. That's all."

Walker grinned. "I don't give a fuck *what* you call it, princess, as long as I can keep kissing you under the mistletoe."

CHAPTER SEVENTEEN

"Who are you?" a small but determined voice demanded.

Walker brushed the snow off his shoulders and stood on the small front porch, looking down at the glowing green lightsaber pointed at his chest. At the other end of it stood a little girl with crazy red curls, dressed in a Snow White costume and black utility belt, complete with grappling hook.

"Um." Walker glanced at the numbers painted next to the door, certain he screwed up the address, but they matched the one Eva had sent him. He was definitely in the right place. "I'm Walker Dunn. I'm here to see Evangeline Bradshaw?"

A dog with a head the size of a small sedan sidled up next to the kid, looking up at Walker like he was waiting for the secret password. Drool hung lazily from the dog's jowls. Walker felt a whoosh of hot breath against his thigh.

Tough crowd.

The little girl finally lowered the lightsaber, her eyes narrowed. "Are you the hockey man?"

Walker smiled, relaxing a little. "Yes, ma'am."

"Mama says you have issues."

"Yeah?" Walker laughed. "What kind of issues?"

"Gracie!" Eva appeared in the doorway, resting her hand tenderly atop the girl's head. "Why don't you go refill Bilbo Baggins's water dish?"

Now the girl smiled, and Walker noticed she was missing two teeth. She was beyond adorable. She waved at Walker, then grabbed the dog by the scruff, leading them deeper into the house.

Walker could barely move. Eva looked... God, she was stunning, her red hair swept off her face, pulled into a loose ponytail that draped over the front of her shoulder. She wore a tight black dress that made her amber eyes stand out like jewels and that would keep Walker up all night long, imagining what it would be like to peel her right out of it.

His dick stirred at the thought.

They held each other's gaze for a minute, breath puffing out in white clouds between them. The sight of her had distracted him from the shock of finding out about the kid, but now Walker blinked, his thoughts returning.

"You have a daughter," he finally said. "And a dog named after a hobbit."

Eva nodded. "Gracie. She's six, going on twenty-five. She named him." Then, softer, "She loves that book."

"She's... she's beautiful, Eva."

A daughter. Of course. Kid had the same red hair. Same amber eyes. The dusting of freckles across her nose was practically a matched set for her mama's. Walker searched his memories, sorting through every conversation he'd ever had with Eva, starting with their very first introduction on the ice.

He was sure she'd never once mentioned a child. He blinked again, trying to make room in his head for this new bit of information. "I can't believe you have a kid."

"Gracie," Eva said again, offering no further explanation. Her jaw jutted out, hands on her hips. It was her battle stance—Walker recognized it immediately.

He wondered if she was testing him, but then she lowered her eyes, her shoulders slumping.

Did I fail? Already?

"I'm sorry," she said softly, holding up her cell phone. "My sister was supposed to babysit, but she just called. She's sick."

"A sister?" *Eva is someone's sister. Eva is someone's mother. Eva has a dog. Eva has a whole entire life that has nothing to do with ice skating. Nothing to do with*

SYLVIA PIERCE

busting his balls. It was stupidly obvious—of course she had a fucking life—but Walker still couldn't process what he'd seen. A daughter. His brain felt slow and sluggish, like his fingers when he skated without gloves. "I mean, is she okay?"

"Sure, just a bug. Probably picked it up from one of her students. Marybeth's a reading specialist. Sorry," Eva said again. She sounded genuinely disappointed, and when she looked up again, she shook her head, regret written all over her face. Stepping back into the small foyer, she started closing the door. "It's probably for the best, anyway. Walker, we really shouldn't—"

"What. Eat dinner together?" He took a step toward the doorway, his eyes locked on hers. "*You're* not sick, right?"

"I don't have a sitter."

"We don't have to go out," Walker said, thinking fast. God, he felt like a schmuck. He hadn't reacted right, hadn't said or done a single thing right since he stepped onto this porch. He didn't want the night to end so early, and especially not like this. "Do either of you have any food allergies? Anything you don't like?"

"Walker, you don't have to—"

"Eva." He stepped fully into the doorway, so close he could smell her honey-vanilla scent, could see the pulse beating beneath the delicate skin of her throat. He brushed

170

the pad of his thumb across her plump lower lip, thrilled that his touch still made her shiver. "You promised me a dinner date. You aren't getting out of it that easy."

A smile finally broke across her face. Walker felt like he'd gotten an early Christmas present.

"It's not a date," she said. "We're team-building."

Walker laughed. "Answer the question, Eva."

"No allergies for either of us," she said. "I don't do olives. Gracie will eat anything."

"And there's no one else in that house I should plan for, right? No other kids, or cousins, or long-lost siblings you forgot to tell me about?"

"Not that I'm aware of."

"What about hobbits? Wizards? Elves?"

Eva smacked his shoulder, and he grabbed her hand, holding it tight. With his free hand he pulled out his phone, scrolled through his contacts, and sent out a quick text.

"What are you up to, forty-six?" she asked.

Walker grinned, pressing a quick kiss to her lips. "Be back in half an hour."

Twenty-six minutes later, the front door swung inward as Walker stomped up the porch stairs with enough takeout to feed the neighborhood. He couldn't see any faces beyond the steaming bags of food in his arms, but he heard everyone crowding at the entrance—

Eva, laughing at the sight of him. Gracie, cheering. Bilbo Baggins, snuffling and panting.

"Where did you get all this?" Eva took the bags off his hands. Walker was thrilled to see that she hadn't changed out of the dress.

"Pasquale's. He's an old friend," he said, hanging his wool coat on a hook by the door. "We grew up together."

"No way!" Gracie beamed. "We love Pasquale's! My favorite is meatball pizza."

"Yep. Everyone loves Pasquale's," Walker said, following Eva into the kitchen. Gracie and Bilbo were right behind him, all of them tumbling into the small room, practically tripping over one another. "But I didn't know what you liked," he said, "so I got a mix of different stuff."

"What stuff?" Gracie asked.

Setting the bags on the kitchen counter, he turned to look at her, her bright eyes beaming with delight. Smiling, he said, "I'm *pretty* sure there's a few slices of meatball pizza in there with your name on it."

"Yesss!" Gracie pumped her fist. Freaking adorable. "What's got *your* name on it?"

"I'm partial to chicken finger subs myself," he said.

Eva laughed, emptying the bags onto the counter behind him. "Looks like you got four of them."

"What, you don't like them?"

"Depends." Eva narrowed her eyes. "With bleu cheese? And hot sauce?"

He pressed a hand to his heart in mock indignation. "What am I, a freaking amateur?"

Eva cracked up. "Apparently not."

She dug out some paper plates and napkins, lit a few candles, then they all loaded up their plates and sat together at the table. It was small and square, tucked into a nook at the end of the kitchen. There wasn't a lot of elbow room, and Walker's knees banged against the table every time he moved, but sitting there with Eva and Gracie, laughing as they all took samples of one another's food, he'd never felt so at home. Where his place was cavernous and sleek and cold, Eva's was cheerful and sunny and lived-in, the way he always thought a real home should be. Gracie's drawings covered the fridge, and the cupboard doors were decorated with paper Santas, snowmen, and gingerbread houses, their edges curling up from what looked like years of use. Every few minutes, Bilbo Baggins would wander through the kitchen, sniff longingly at the table, and then move on, nails clicking softly on the linoleum.

Walker was glad Eva's sister had canceled.

"Mr. Dunn?" Gracie asked suddenly.

He smiled at her across the table. "You can call me Walker."

"Okay." Nodding, she set down her half-eaten slice of

pizza and looked up at Walker expectantly. Seriously. "Walker?"

Walker took a deep breath, waiting for her to ask something mortifying or impossible, like *why do you keep staring at Mommy like you want to eat her?* Or *Do you know that my daddy can kick your butt?* Or *Where do babies come from?*

"Who do you think would win in a cage match—Snow White or Luke Skywalker?"

Eva burst out laughing. "That's my daughter, everyone. Sugar and spice."

Walker grabbed a napkin and blotted the hot sauce from around his mouth, considering. "Luke the farm boy, or Luke the Jedi?"

"Jedi."

Walker crumpled up his napkin. "Snow White. She's a total badass. I mean, butt. Total badbutt."

"Luke has The Force," Gracie said. "*And* a lightsaber."

"True, but my girl Snow White is resourceful. She can talk to animals, she knows how to survive in the woods, *and* she knows how to put up with seven dudes. Can you imagine how many dirty socks they left? Not to mention never putting down the toilet seat. And you might be too young to realize this, Gracie, but let me tell you something about boys."

The girl's amber eyes widened, and Walker leaned in

conspiratorially, whispering behind his hand. "We stink like farm animals. You should definitely stay away from us until you're at least forty."

"Forty-five," Eva said.

Gracie cracked up, and Walker was damn near ready to make it his life's mission to keep that gap-toothed smile on her face for all eternity.

"Did you know in the *real* Snow White," Gracie continued, dunking a carrot stick into a tub of bleu cheese dressing, "the evil queen tries to kill her a whole bunch of times?" She was breathless with excitement, her red curls bouncing. "But at the end the queen goes to Snow White's wedding to the prince and they make her wear red-hot iron shoes and dance around in them until her feet burn up and she dies." She smiled brightly, then popped the carrot into her mouth.

Walker raised a brow. "I… No. I didn't know that. Thank you for enlightening me."

"Gracie, you are the creepiest child ever." Eva cracked up. "Who raised you?"

Gracie rolled her eyes, a move straight out of her mother's playbook. Walker caught Eva's gaze and smiled, squeezing her knee under the table. He wondered if Eva even realized how alike she and her daughter were.

"I saw it on a documentary at Aunt Marybeth's," Gracie said. "All the fairytales are like that. In Cinderella, the step-sisters cut off their own toes and left blood all over the glass slipper."

"We're eating!" Eva said, but she was laughing.

"Well, all the more reason I'm sticking with my original answer," Walker said, stealing a chicken wing from Eva's plate. "Snow White is a survivor. My money's on her."

Gracie looked down at her dress, considering. "Maybe you're right."

"But that doesn't mean you can't pack a lightsaber for backup," Walker added.

"And a grappling hook?" Gracie asked.

"Also very handy," Walker agreed.

"Hey," Eva said to Gracie, her eyes sparkling in the candlelight. "Think you can grapple with clearing the table? I'd say we're about done with dinner."

Walker stood up to help, unsure what was supposed to happen next. All he knew was that he wasn't ready for the night to end. He wanted to spend more time with them. With *both* of them. He was still processing the fact that Eva had a kid, that she hadn't told him about her, that he was here, now, hanging out with the two of them, seeing Eva in a whole new light. He was still getting to know her as a skater and coach, as his lover. And now he wanted to know her as a mother, too—a realization that nearly knocked him on his ass.

So when the table had been cleared and the last of the

leftovers tucked into the fridge and Eva looked up at him with those bright golden eyes and said, "Who wants dessert?" Walker didn't even bother hiding his dopey-ass grin.

He knew it was crazy, getting tangled up like this. Reckless, even. But he no longer cared. Two hours in this home with Eva and Gracie, and he was a goner for them both.

CHAPTER EIGHTEEN

Eva felt like she was in high school again. Her stomach was fizzy, her cheeks hurt from smiling, and she could barely keep up with her sister's frantic texts.

She'd made the mistake of texting Marybeth after Walker had gone out to pick up the food, and Marybeth had been texting for updates approximately every four minutes since.

Now, Eva sent Walker and Gracie into the living room to relax while she dished up gingerbread ice cream and tried to catch up with Marybeth's demanding texts.

Her phone buzzed again. *EVA! What is happening over there?*

I'm in the kitchen getting dessert, she replied. *W&G are hanging out in the living room.*

What are they doing?

Eva didn't actually know. She couldn't see the living

room from the kitchen, but she heard them laughing, and figured that was a good sign. She crept out of the kitchen and took a peek.

OMG, she texted Marybeth. *He's reading to Gracie on the couch.*

What book?

Does it matter?

Paint the picture for me, Eva.

Eva paused to listen, then texted back, *The Hobbit. OMG, he's totally doing the voices. All of them.*

What voices?

Like hobbits and wizards and everyone. Eva's heart skipped every time Walker read another line, every time he made her daughter laugh. Gracie had always been a happy kid, despite some of the challenges they'd faced. But it'd been a long time since Eva had heard Gracie truly crack up—the kind of laugh that made your eyes water, your stomach hurt.

Until now, she hadn't realized how much she'd missed that sound. How much she'd longed to make it herself.

The phone buzzed again in her hand. *You are in so much trouble.*

Can't talk, Eva replied. *Ovaries melting. Send ambulance.*

!!! You need an intervention, not an ambulance!

They're seriously melting, Marybeth. I can't even deal with this level of sweetness right now.

It wasn't much of an exaggeration. Crazy as it was, the sight of that impossibly sexy badass Buffalo Tempest center scrunching up his face and talking like a hobbit while her daughter sat next to him on the couch, utterly enraptured, was enough to make her—for the first time since Gracie was born—think about having more kids.

That thought should've scared Eva straight—should've had her ushering Walker right out the front door, banished with all thoughts of more children and family and a settled-down kind of life. Instead, it made her heart beat with new life.

Marybeth buzzed in again, and Eva headed back to the kitchen, leaving Walker and Gracie alone in Middle Earth.

EVA! You are not allowed to get attached!

Eva's reply was automatic—*I'm not!*—but it was also, Eva had realized the instant she hit send, pure bullshit.

She *was* getting attached. Hell, she'd moved past attached a long time ago. This? This odd thumping in her chest? The butterflies flitting around in her stomach? The laughter bubbling up from deep down inside, just waiting to burst out? The way her skin heated at his touch? The way her thighs clenched with just one look from those deep, soulful eyes?

Yes, Eva was pretty sure there was a word for all that... but it *wasn't* attachment.

She looked down at the screen, fingers hovering over the letters, not sure what to tell Marybeth. Not even sure what to tell herself.

Was it even possible? Was she actually... was she *falling* for Walker Dunn?

"I hope that's not your wingman on the phone." Walker's voice, soft and warm on the back of her neck, made her jump. She dropped the phone on the counter and whirled around to face him.

He was close, his eyes full of desire, his breath tickling her lips. Their bodies pressed together, *fit* together, warmth seeking warmth. Eva slid her hands up the front of his shirt, the crisp white button-down he'd put on for their date now rumpled and covered with dog hair. She fisted it in her hands, feeling his heart pounding beneath the fabric.

"You're already home, Eva," he said, his voice a sexy, sultry whisper, so intimate in her tiny kitchen. "So if you want to get out of this date, you have to convince *me* to leave." Walker put his hands on the counter on either side of her, caging her in. "And it won't be easy. I like it here. *Really* like it."

She was paralyzed in his arms, unable to move, unable to speak, unable to blink.

Walker leaned forward, his lips brushing her ear, her neck, the hollow of her throat. "Damn, you smell good, woman. I don't know how much longer I can keep my hands off you." His teeth grazed the sensitive skin where her shoulder met her neck, and she felt her nipples harden, aching for the bite and caress of his mouth. Eva had thought the other times they'd been together had been so perfect, so hot, but now she knew they'd only been a prequel, too short, too fast. Her legs trembled as she imagined taking him to her bedroom tonight, locking the door, letting herself be devoured hour after agonizingly sweet hour.

Walker slid his thigh between her legs, her dress hiking up, everything in her wound tight, desperate for his touch...

"Walker," she whispered, the ache between her thighs growing deeper. Her eyelids fluttered closed, and she pulled him closer, tasting the barest brush of his lips as he kissed her...

"Mama!" Gracie shouted from the living room. "Where's our ice cream?"

Eva opened her eyes, but Walker didn't pull away. Not yet.

He smiled, and nipped again at her neck, her earlobe, his voice thick with desire. "To be continued, princess."

"Your daughter gave me homework," Walker said.

Eva had just gotten Gracie tucked into bed, and now

she took a seat on the couch next to Walker, glad to see that he'd started a fire.

"Do I even want to know?" Eva asked.

"I made the mistake of admitting I'd never read *The Hobbit* before—just saw the movie."

"Oh, no." Eva laughed. Gracie was a purist. Eva had rented *The Hobbit* DVDs for her last year, and the kid turned it off fifteen minutes in, utterly disgusted. Later that night, Eva had found her under her blanket with a flashlight, paging through the book she couldn't quite read on her own. *I just need to wash that movie out of my brain, Mama.*

Walker nodded at the book, stacked on the coffee table with a few others Eva recognized as Gracie's favorites. "The kid says I have to read them all, *and* do a one-page book report on my favorite one."

Eva laughed. "Did she give you a deadline?"

"New Year's Day."

"Friendly advice? Don't miss it."

"Wouldn't dream of disappointing her," Walker said. "Or getting my ass kicked. Hell, Eva. She definitely has your spark."

Eva rested her head on Walker's shoulder, enjoying the warmth of his breath stirring her hair. The fire crackled before them, wrapping Eva in a sense of warmth and safety that had been missing from her life for a long time.

She hadn't planned on introducing Walker and Gracie tonight. She was supposed to be rushing out the door when Walker arrived, Gracie and Marybeth tucked safely inside, unheard and unseen. But now she was glad plans had changed.

"I've never seen her get attached to anyone so quickly," Eva said. "She… she has a hard time trusting people. Especially men-people."

Walker shifted beside her, and Eva knew what he was going to say even before the words were out. "What about her—"

"Her father isn't in the picture," she said, looking up at him. "His choice." His *insistence* was more like it, but Eva bit her bottom lip. She'd already said too much. She hated talking about him. Hated thinking about him. The only reason she didn't hate *him* was that he'd given her Gracie, and she just couldn't find it in her heart to despise the father of the child who'd lit up Eva's entire life.

"I can't…" Walker's jaw ticked, his eyes flashing with anger. "I can't imagine having a kid like Gracie, and not wanting to be part of her life." The emotion in his eyes surprised her. For Eva, the sun rose and set on Gracie, but Walker had just met her. Up until tonight, she wasn't even sure if he liked children. But now, that look in his eyes… it wasn't just anger. It was heartache. For her. For Gracie.

Eva's heart hammered in her throat, and she shifted to the other end of the couch, tucking her feet up under her legs. "Wow. It's possible I'm the worst first date ever."

"Oh, we're calling this a date now?" Walker flashed a grin, his eyes sparkling in the firelight. "I thought we were team-building."

"You *did* help me do the dishes. That counts."

"Yes, throwing paper plates into the trash was a valiant effort on my part. Thank God I was here to share the burden."

"You also made dinner," she added, nudging his thigh with her foot. "And then my daughter gave you homework, and I started talking about my ex." Eva shook her head, not sure whether to be amused or embarrassed. "You're probably counting the seconds until you can make your escape. I'm surprised *your* wingman hasn't called."

"Oh, they did. Both of them."

"Let me guess. Roscoe and Henny?"

Walker nodded. "I told them to fuck off, then turned off my phone."

"That was pretty brave of you, forty-six. What happens if the date turns *really* bad and you need an out?"

"Not a chance, princess." He grabbed her foot, took it into his lap. With a near-orgasmic touch, he pressed his thumb into her arch, massaging away the tension. With every stroke, shockwaves of pleasure radiated up and down her legs, her spine, all the way across her scalp.

"Whatever you're doing, I'll spoon feed you gingerbread ice cream every day for a month if you promise not to stop touching me."

"Done and done." He slid his hand up her calf, her thigh, caressing her bare skin. Eva slid her other leg across his lap, grateful she hadn't changed out of the dress.

Eva's eyes drifted closed as she lost herself beneath his strong, capable hands, her body melting at his touch, craving more of him, all of him.

"There's a game tomorrow night," he said, his voice like warm honey. "I'd really love it if you and Gracie would come."

"A Tempest game?" she asked, even though the answer was obvious.

"I've got good seats. I know a few of the higher-ups."

Eva laughed, her reservations ebbing away. It'd been ages since she'd been to a game, and Gracie had never even seen one on television. It might actually be fun. Besides, she'd broken so many of her rules already— hockey boys, intimacy, bringing a man into her home, getting attached—standing on principle over a simple hockey game seemed a little ridiculous.

"Sounds like fun," she said. "Count us in."

Walker shifted, and then she felt the press of soft lips on her knee, slowly fluttering upward. His fingers brushed the hem of her dress, pushing it up to reveal her bare thighs. Instinctively, she spread her legs, urging him closer, unable to resist her body's own desperate pleas.

When she opened her eyes, Walker was leaning over her, the look in his eyes hungry. Feral.

"I've been waiting all night to touch you," he said, brushing her lips with a powder-soft kiss. "To taste you." Another kiss, another soft moan. "To make you come."

He was rock hard beneath his dark jeans, the press of him sending a thrill to her core.

With trembling fingers, she unbuttoned his shirt, sliding her hands down the front of his perfectly sculpted chest, the firm ridges of his abs contracting at her touch. He was all muscle and heat and power, and Eva ached to feel him inside her, to feel the red-hot pulse of him as they brought each other over the edge.

Walker lowered his body on to hers, the solid weight comforting and delicious, the pressure between her thighs driving her wild. The button of his jeans dug into her stomach, but Eva didn't care. She wanted more. She arched her hips, desperate to feel the grind of his rock-hard cock.

"Evangeline…" He nipped her ear, his breath hot on her flesh, the sound of her full name on his lips making her wet.

"Don't wake Gracie," she whispered, barely getting the words out.

"Oh, I can be quiet, princess," he said, tracing a slow circle over her nipple. God, she wanted out of this dress. His touch was killing her. "But as we know, you're a bit of a screamer."

Eva bolted up. "What? I am *so* not a—"

Before she could respond, he smothered her with a kiss, pushing her back down against the couch. She parted her lips, gasping for air as he claimed her mouth again and again, teeth clashing, breath hot and needy, stubble scratching her chin, and all she could think was *more*. More. More. More. She wanted him with a fiery, desperate need she felt in her blood, in her bones.

Frantically she reached for his waistband, fumbling with the button and zipper, sliding her hand inside and fisting his smooth, perfect cock. It was bigger than she'd remembered, the satin-smooth skin hot to the touch, pulsing as she stroked him.

"Eva, you... you have to... slow..." Walker finally grabbed her hand, forcing her to stop. "Five more seconds and I would've lost it."

She leaned forward and bit his bottom lip, sucking gently. "So lose it," she whispered. "Let me make you come."

"I..." Walker closed his eyes, shaking his head as if he were trying to clear his thoughts. When he looked at her again, his eyes were dark, hooded. Eva could see the pulse jumping at his throat. "Not yet," he said, a slow smile curving his lips. "We've got all night, and I intend to make the most of every single—"

Bilbo Baggins let out a woof, pressing his cold wet nose against her foot. Eva yelped. "Bilbo Baggins!" She laughed. "Go away!"

He snuffled around the couch, lingering. Eva scratched behind his ears. "Aww, I know you're just looking out for me, you big lug."

Walker laughed. "Bilbo Baggins is trying to cockblock me."

"He's protective."

"Hmm." Walker raised a brow, teasing her lips with another kiss. In a husky voice that sent a fresh shock to her core, he said, "Think you're in danger, Evangeline?"

Her name melted on his tongue, his breath warm on her lips, and *oh God yes*. Yes, she was absolutely in danger, every warning sign in her body lighting up, flashing, howling to get her attention.

But she ignored them all. Even Bilbo Baggins, her very last line of defense. Her hand drifted away from the dog, and soon she lost track of him altogether. Lost track of the fire, burning down low. Lost track of time and space and the sound of her own heartbeat.

She was gone, her body turning into jelly as Walker slid his fingers between her thighs, inside her, deep, deeper, slow and perfect, then fast and hard, hitting her just exactly right.

Eva's eyes rolled back in her head, her body writhing in pleasure—not just from what he was doing to her, but from what she knew was still to come.

Their previous encounters notwithstanding, Eva could tell that Walker was a man who preferred to take his time in the bedroom. Who would work on discovering and mastering her pleasures with the same intense commitment he showed on the ice. Dedicated and driven. Strong and powerful. And *all* man.

Her thighs trembled in anticipation as Walker ran his nose along her jaw, her neck, his fingers sliding out of her and groping for the zipper at the back of her dress.

She missed his touch. Needed him back there. Now.

"Don't stop," she said, breathing hard.

"Believe me, I'm just getting started." He tugged the dress down to expose her breasts, sucking one of her nipples into his mouth, his fingers sliding blissfully inside her once again. He found the perfect rhythm, stroking her, his teeth and tongue teasing her sensitive nipple into a stiff peak, every single nerve ending in her body on absolute fire for this man, for his touch, for his kiss...

"Walker, I'm close. Don't stop. Don't—"

"Santa?"

The tiny, sleepy voice floated in from the hallway, and Eva and Walker froze.

"Shit," Eva mouthed, her breathing still ragged.

"Double shit." Walker laughed silently, sliding back to the end of the couch with as much stealth as he could muster.

Eva was grateful the back of the couch blocked most of Gracie's view.

"It's okay," she called out. "It's just us. Go back to bed, baby."

"But I thought I heard Santa."

"No, sweetie," Eva said. "It was probably just… Bilbo Baggins."

The dog yelped at the sound of his name, darting out from behind the Christmas tree. Eva hadn't even seen him hiding back there.

"Definitely not Santa," Walker said. His shirt was buttoned up again, and he leaned his elbows on the back of the couch, smiling at Gracie. "I know for a fact that he operates on a strict schedule. Christmas is still, what? Six months away?"

Gracie giggled. "Nineteen days and nine hours and thirty-two minutes."

"Oh, three months and four days, you say?"

"No!"

"Twelve years and seventy-eight days?" Walker teased.

More giggles. "Walker! Don't say that, or Santa will put you on the naughty list."

"He's already on the naughty list," Eva mumbled, trying to wriggle back into her dress without totally cracking up at their predicament. They really needed to relocate to her bedroom.

Finally put back together, she rose from the couch, shooting him a look that said, *don't you dare move.* "Be right back."

Eva tucked Gracie back into bed, bribed Bilbo Baggins to stay in the kitchen with a few of his favorite dog biscuits, then headed back toward the living room. Walker had put another log on the fire and returned to the couch, one arm extended over the back. It was the perfect spot, made just for her, and it called to her like a beacon.

But she lingered in the space that separated the living and dining rooms, scared and uncertain. For all of her talk, all of her desire, all of the things they'd already done tonight... deep down Eva knew that sleeping with Walker again would only complicate things.

For both of them.

He looked up at her as she finally entered the room, the look in his eyes unreadable. She sensed he had the same reservations. Things had already heated up too fast.

"Everything okay with Gracie?" he asked.

Eva sat in the rocking chair across from the couch. "She wants to know if the hockey man knows how to make pancakes."

Walker raised a brow, and only then did Eva realize what she'd implied.

"Walker..." She closed her eyes, hating the conflicted tone in her voice. Why couldn't she just enjoy this? They were two consenting adults. They were insanely attracted to each other. They knew how to make each other feel good even more than they knew how to drive each other crazy on the ice.

Eva stood, forcing a smile. She wanted to hold out her hand, lead him back to her bedroom. She wanted to lock the door and strip him bare and spend all the hours until sunrise making love to this sinfully hot, impossibly sweet man whose touch lit up her insides.

But she couldn't. Her legs felt like rubber, her nerves overloaded with sensations, her brain and her heart locked in that endless battle she wasn't sure either side would ever win.

Why was life so damn complicated?

Why was Eva *making* it so damn complicated?

Walker finally rose from the couch, his smile sincere, but unable to mask the disappointment in his eyes. "I... should probably head out," he said, saving her the awkwardness of making the excuse herself. She could've kissed him for that. She *wanted* to kiss him for it, but then they'd be right back on the couch, or in her bedroom, and that was just a bad idea any way she looked at it.

Wasn't it?

"Walker, maybe—"

"I have a meeting with Gallagher first thing tomorrow," he said.

Eva nodded, hating the burn in her cheeks. No, this was for the best. They had to back off a little. At least for tonight, before things progressed. "Me too," she said. "I mean, I have back-to-back clients in the morning."

"Not hockey players, I hope?"

"Two former ballerinas training for an ice show, one senior citizens class, and a five-year-old whose mother insists is the next Michelle Kwan."

Walker laughed. "Is she?"

"Poor kid would rather be home drinking hot cocoa and watching cartoons."

"Can't blame her," Walker said, retrieving his coat from the hook. Then, with a wink, "The ice is a cruel mistress."

All the unspoken things hung between them in the air, frozen, but if there was a right response to that, Eva couldn't find it.

She stuck her feet into the snow boots by the door and walked him out onto the porch. It was still snowing, big, fat flakes that drifted to the ground in an endless ballet. Somewhere in the distance, a train whistled—the only sound for miles and miles. Eva's skin erupted in goose bumps.

The blast of cold air should've snapped her back to reality, cleared her thoughts, made her grateful that she and Walker had avoided disaster. But instead it only made her feel cold and lonely. Full of regret. Sad in a way she couldn't quite place.

"Bet this non-date didn't turn out like you thought it would," she said finally, forcing a laugh.

Walker's eyes narrowed, still sparkling with mischief and desire. "You're a woman of mystery and intrigue, Evangeline. I'll say that much."

She leaned forward and kissed his cheek, trying to memorize the smell of his skin, uncertain what their next meeting would hold.

"See you tomorrow," he said, tentative. "For the game?"

Eva nodded, and she swore he exhaled with relief. "And then again on Wednesday for another practice," she said.

"Admit it," he said. "You can't get enough of me."

Eva laughed, the sound swallowed up by the snowy night. "No."

"No, you won't admit it, or no, you can't get enough?"

"Good *night*, Walker." She pressed a final kiss to his

lips, and then closed the door, afraid to look into his eyes again.

Afraid of what she might find there.

Afraid that it might mirror her own impossible feelings.

But mostly, afraid that it wouldn't.

CHAPTER NINETEEN

Eva hadn't seen Gracie this excited since she discovered the original *Twilight Zone* series on Netflix at Aunt Marybeth's.

The kid had been chattering nonstop since Walker picked them up for the game, and now that they were here at the arena, her excitement levels were reaching core meltdown levels. She could barely keep her smile in check, bouncing on her toes with every step, asking a million questions, never loosening her grip on Walker's hand.

Admittedly, Eva was pretty excited herself. She hadn't been to a game in years, but now, as Walker led them through the crowd toward their suite, all the old feelings were coming back. She smiled, wondering what her father would think about the new uniforms—they were red and black when he'd died, not blue and silver like they were now. The arena had changed, too—the old one had been torn down, rebuilt—huge and modern and clean, with a vast sea of dark blue seats that rose like waves in the ocean. But other than that, the important stuff was all the same: the gleam of the pre-game ice, unmarred by a single blade. The singsong calls of the hotdog and popcorn vendors that walked the aisles. The energy of the crowd as they filled in the seats, everyone eager to root for the home team.

The place had a heartbeat all its own, and Eva felt it—that pulse, that hum, an undercurrent that buzzed through everything, not so different from the buzz she used to feel at her own skating events.

She missed her father with a deep ache, but it made her smile anyway. He would've loved Walker.

"Here's our stop," Walker said, leading them inside a luxury suite that looked down over center ice.

It was similar to the one she and Walker had stumbled into in their practice arena yesterday, only much larger, and packed full of people. The thick carpet beneath her feet was the same color, and the moment she'd stepped on it, her cheeks flamed.

Are those mistletoe... You have no idea how bad I want you... Fucking hell, Eva...

She took a deep breath, distracting herself by checking out the other guests—mostly men in suits, a few younger kids in hockey jerseys, a handful of nicely dressed women that Eva guessed were wives or other family members of the team. Doug McKellen was there, too, but before Eva could catch his eye, he was drawn into a conversation with a couple of men Eva recognized from her first day on the ice with Walker—she thought one was the general manager.

"You good?" Walker slid his hand behind her, resting it on her lower back. It was warm and solid and familiar, a touch she wanted to keep all to herself.

Eva met his eyes and smiled, her soft sigh inaudible in the crowded room. As much as she hated the idea of sharing Walker with a room full of strangers, it was probably best that they weren't left alone tonight.

Dangerous things happened when they were left alone.

"Mama, did you ever get to go to a hockey game before?" Gracie asked. She was sitting between Walker and Eva at the high-backed barstools right up front, best seats in the house. Walker's arm was draped over the back of Gracie's stool, and every few minutes his fingers brushed Eva's shoulder, sending a shock of warmth down her arm.

"Your grandpa used to take me all the time when I was your age," Eva replied, ignoring the familiar guilt that crawled up her spine whenever she thought about hockey games and Gracie—specifically, Gracie's father.

A couple of years ago, she'd told Gracie the basics about him, but she'd left out most of the details—his career, how he and Eva had met, what he'd actually said when he'd found out about his daughter.

She wondered now if bringing Gracie tonight had been a mistake. If letting Walker into her life—into *both* of their lives—would end up hurting her in some deep, devastating way that Eva wouldn't be able to fix.

But despite Eva's dark thoughts, Gracie only smiled, her amber eyes bright and content. "Well, I'm glad that Walker can take us now instead, because grandpa's dead, you know."

Walker's eyes went wide, but Eva was already laughing so hard, several of the other guests had turned to look at her.

"You know something, honeybee?" Eva ran a hand over Gracie's red curls. "I like your style."

"What's my style?" she asked, but before Eva could answer, the lights flashed overhead, and the booming voice of the announcer echoed through the stadium.

"Game time," Walker said, and Gracie cheered, clapping for the team as they skated out onto the rink.

"Are those your friends down there?" Gracie asked. Walker had explained to her on the drive over about his injury—that he couldn't play tonight, but wanted Eva and Gracie to be here to help him root for the team and support his friends.

"Sure are," Walker said. "Roscoe and Henny are starters—numbers thirty-eight and nineteen, left and right wings. See?" He pointed down at center ice, and Gracie nodded. "The guy in the middle—seventeen? Lance Fahey—the guys call him Sir Lancelot. He's our starting center."

Eva's throat tightened. Walker's tone was light and jovial, but Eva could sense the strain in his voice, could see the slight bend in his otherwise straight shoulders when he talked about the starting center. Though Walker had never mentioned him by name, Eva knew that Fahey was the young kid currently playing Walker's position. That he—if Eva didn't do her job right—might even replace Walker permanently.

Her heart ached for Walker; she wanted him to succeed so, so badly. He didn't belong in this suite with all these fancy people, most of them not even paying attention to the game. He belonged out there on the ice, playing the game he loved. He belonged with his teammates, speeding down to the goal zone in a cold fury, slapping that puck home.

Eva couldn't imagine what it would do to him if he never got that chance.

No. We're not going to let that happen…

"Does Sir Lancelot have a sword?" Gracie wanted to know.

"Excellent question." Walker laughed. "I'll ask him. Okay, they're about to drop the puck. Don't blink—otherwise you might miss it."

Gracie propped her elbows on the bar and leaned forward, completely captivated.

Down on the ice, the starters for both teams lined up with their sticks for the face-off, all muscle and attitude and fierce, terrifying determination. Eva leaned forward, too, unable to resist the pull of their raw, competitive energy.

The puck hit the center line in a blur, sticks clashing as the men fought for control.

The crowd cheered as Roscoe took it down the ice. He tapped it over to Fahey, who passed it to Henny, then it was back in Fahey's control as the three of them charged into Colorado Wolves territory, a single, menacing unit. The puck slid to Henny, then back over to Roscoe, who tapped it seamlessly into the net.

First goal of the game, less than a minute in. Everyone in the stands was on their feet, whooping and hollering.

"Yes! *That's* how it's done!" Walker gave Gracie a high-five, and she pumped her fist, imitating him perfectly.

Eva tried to focus on the game, but seeing her

daughter so happy, so unburdened, Eva couldn't stop watching her. Couldn't stop sneaking glances at Walker, the same questions echoing through her head.

What if this is real? What if it doesn't have to end?

No, it had to end. Eva was certain of that. If not because of her pending relocation, then for the simple fact that she couldn't allow herself to fall for him. To get complacent. To put herself in a position where he could hurt her. Where he could hurt either of them.

Eva turned back to the game. Roscoe and Henny were dominating the ice, ducking and dodging, the puck a black blur as they sped toward the goal line. Henny took the shot, shooting the puck right over the goalie's shoulder, and in it went. The crowd roared, the energy surging through the stadium in excited waves.

Gracie had a million questions, every second of the game, and Walker never once faltered in his answers, never once dismissed her. The two of them had a natural bond, one Eva had never seen Gracie share with anyone other than herself and Marybeth—not with any of Gracie's teachers, or neighbors, or babysitters, or even her own friends. And Walker... his whole face lit up when either Gracie or Eva smiled his way.

The questions fluttered through her mind again.

What if this is real? What if it doesn't have to end?

Eva sighed. No. It was just a fairytale. It wasn't real. It never could be.

At the end of the first period, Gracie hopped off her stool to use the private bathroom in the suite. Walker slid onto Gracie's spot and leaned in close, his lips brushing Eva's neck. "You okay?"

Eva nodded, but her insides were a jumbled mess, all crossed wires and dizzy butterflies at his touch. His proximity. His mint-and-wood-smoke scent. She didn't have words to describe what she was feeling, exactly, but that didn't make it any less all-consuming and dangerous. Any less real, no matter what the logical side of her mind kept insisting.

The way he'd made her feel on their bench that day had changed her, inside and out, whether she wanted to admit it or not. The way she'd felt in his arms again last night... The way she'd dreamed of him almost every night since they'd met, waking herself up with her hands between her thighs, her body trembling as if he'd been in her bed... The lurch in her stomach when he looked at her like that—like he was doing right now—that was *all* real.

Maybe she could've walked away after that first time. Could've chalked it up to sexual attraction, loneliness, the aching need for physical contact she'd denied herself for so long. She could've wrapped that up with a nice little bow, thanked him for giving her that exquisite release, and moved on with her life.

But she hadn't. And every time she saw him, a little piece of that ice wall around her heart started to melt.

"Are you having fun?" Walker asked.

"Yes. This… this is amazing."

He tapped his lips, considering. "Are the seats okay?"

"Obviously."

He leaned in close again, knees brushing her thigh, his voice low and sexy. "Is it your date? Because *something's* got your mind working overtime. I can smell the smoke."

Eva held his gaze, the truth balanced on her tongue like a caught snowflake.

Yes, it's my date, Walker. It's the way you look at me. It's the way you make me feel when I'm with you. It's the fact that I hardly know you, yet it feels like we've been friends for an age. I can't stop wanting you, replaying your every kiss, your every touch, your every whisper against my skin. If I spend any more time with you, I'm going to fall, and it's going to hurt.

But instead, all she said was, "Yes, it's totally my date. Maybe you could kick his ass for me."

"Maybe *you* could kick his ass. Or just spank him." Walker arched a dark brow, the playful spark in his steel-gray eyes drawing Eva closer. She rested her hand on his thigh, leaning forward, her lips grazing the rough, stubbled edge of his jaw—

"I'm hungry." Gracie popped up between them,

bouncing on her toes again, and Eva pulled back, finally remembering where they were.

Walker nodded toward a spread of appetizers set up at the back. "Did you see anything good on the table over there?"

Gracie shook her head, her nose crinkling. "Just fancy things and vegetables."

"Gross," Walker said. "No hotdogs, then?"

"Only the little ones with toothpicks."

Walker rose from the chair. "I think it's time for a hotdog run. Sound good for everyone?"

Eva nodded. It *did* sound good, actually. She loved stadium dogs, fully loaded, the messier the better. She couldn't even remember the last time she ate one, but her mouth was already watering.

"Can I come, too?" Gracie asked, grabbing Walker's hand.

Walker looked at Eva and smiled. The two of them could do puppy-dog eyes better than Bilbo Baggins, and they were totally teaming up on her now. How could she say no?

"Sure," she said, laughing. "But hold Walker's hand and don't wander off."

Left alone at the bar, Eva was lost in the storm of her own thoughts. Why did Walker have to be so damn charming? Why did Gracie have to like him so much? Why did *Eva* have to like him so much?

Her eyes were drifting lazily over the players down on the ice, her brain barely registering the plays, when she felt a hand on her shoulder. She looked up to find Doug McKellen grinning at her warmly.

"So our boy finally brought you to a game," he said, chuckling. "Mind if I sit? I've been trying to get over here to say hello for an hour."

Eva gestured to the stool next to her. "I saw you when we arrived, but you looked like you were in a meeting."

"Busted." He smiled, the skin around his kind eyes crinkling. "When you love your job, it's hard to leave it at the office."

Eva nodded. She could relate—in more ways than one. It was part of the reason she'd been so intrigued by his offer. The chance to continue skating, coaching—and making a full-time salary? It was almost too good to be true.

"Where is forty-six, anyway?" he asked, looking around.

"Hotdog run."

"Don't blame him. I can't even identify half the stuff they have on that buffet."

"My daughter felt the same way."

McKellen nodded, but his eyes were serious now. Lowering his voice, he said, "I understand you're making some nice progress with him, Miss Bradshaw."

Eva nodded, relaying some of Walker's recent drill

times. "He's already getting stronger, really pushing himself during our sessions. I think you'll be pleased with the end results."

"We met with Walker today," McKellen said. "Whatever you're doing? Keep it up. It's not just his times that have improved. Gallagher says he hasn't seen him in such good spirits in a long time."

"Really? That's great to hear," Eva said.

Walker hadn't said much about the time he spent with his coach and trainers on days when he and Eva weren't working together, but she knew that he still attended some of the team practices and staff meetings, keeping the coach updated on his progress. She was glad for the compliment.

"Gallagher and the managers are really impressed." McKellen chuckled again, but this time it felt tight, almost forced. With a wink, he said, "If I don't watch my back, they're liable to steal you away from me."

"What do you mean?" she asked, puzzled, but McKellen's face had changed again, back to light and jovial.

"Have you given any more thought to my offer?" he asked.

"Lots," she admitted.

"I was thinking we should fly you out to Minnesota early in the new year," he said, "give us a chance to show you around the facility, introduce you to the staff.

They're eager to meet you, and of course they can answer any questions you might have."

"Oh, I... sure. That would be great." Eva's head was spinning again. Fly her out there? She hadn't even accepted yet.

"Aw, hell. Where are my manners?" He rose from the stool, shaking his head, his smile back in place. "When I saw you sitting over here, I promised myself I would just say hi, not give you the hard sell."

"That's okay. I appreciate your enthusiasm."

"It's not every day you get the chance to recruit a world champion figure skater, Miss Bradshaw." McKellen nodded toward the ice, where a fight had just broken out against the boards. "These teams are getting stronger, tougher, harder to beat every year. But they're not necessarily getting better at skating. With you on board, I think we can put together some real innovative programs."

Something fluttered in Eva's chest. It was hard not to get caught up in McKellen's plans, to imagine what it would be like to build something from the ground up like that.

"I'm definitely considering it," she said again. "It sounds like an amazing opportunity."

Walker and Gracie were back, carrying a tray of hotdogs and sodas. A new Tempest ball cap sat on Gracie's head, the wide brim hiding her eyes.

"Well, I'll leave you guys to it." McKellen smiled, clapping Walker on the shoulder. To Eva, he said, "Miss Bradshaw, you've got my number."

Walker set down the food and helped Gracie onto the stool. "What was that all about?" he asked Eva. "Wait, let me guess: you told him you wanted to give back all the money he paid you because spending time on the ice with me is its own reward."

"Are you kidding? I told him you're such a pain in the butt, I'm tripling my rates."

The hotdogs were just as disgustingly awesome as Eva remembered, and she wolfed down two of them in the time it took Walker's boys to score another goal.

But despite her efforts to focus on the game, to laugh and relax and forget about job offers and money and broken hearts, Eva's worries kept creeping right in, storm clouds gathering over an otherwise perfect outing.

The initial excitement from her conversation with McKellen had faded, leaving her rattled and tense. It was a cold reminder of just how much was at stake here—of just how dangerous her flirty little game with Walker really was. Not just for Eva and her job prospects. Not even for her heart.

But for Walker.

This was his future. His career. His life. She couldn't let him risk it for her no more than she could risk her own future for him.

The realization came over her like an icy wind, cold and severe, leaving her chilled and sad in a way she didn't fully understand. No matter how charming he was, no matter how hot, how funny, how sexy, how kind... no. None of it mattered. Eva had to stop the mental tug-of-war, stop her own mixed signals and crazy desires. They had their fun, but playtime was over. She had to get their relationship back on the right track—the *professional* track—before the thin ice beneath their feet shattered.

CHAPTER TWENTY

Walker slammed into the boards, his shoulder taking the brunt of the impact before he dropped to the ice. Pain shot through his arm, so hot and bright it made his vision blur.

Motherfucker.

It was his third wipeout in an hour, each one tearing into his ego as ferociously as it did his body.

Walker wanted to be grateful it was the shoulder and not the knee, but that gratitude was fleeting. His knee was stiff and swollen; favoring it is what had thrown off his balance today, sent him sliding into the boards. He'd been tossing and turning all week, the pain in his knee so bad it woke him up at night.

He was overdoing it, downplaying his doctor's warnings, hoping that working it harder would help him strengthen the muscles around it. And he didn't know how to admit it to Eva.

He didn't want to disappoint her.

"You okay?" Eva held out a hand to help him up, but he waved it off, hauling himself back up. Eva scanned him head to toe, then back up again, finally settling on his eyes. The look she gave him wasn't pity. Wasn't even concern. It was anger. "What the hell is going on with you, forty-six?"

"I don't know," he snapped. "What's it say on your little clipboard?"

She didn't respond. Just stared at him, hard and unmoving. He used to think that particular glare was her go-to look, but now he realized it was just one of many in her arsenal, each one as layered and nuanced as the shades of honey in her eyes.

Today's look was the *I'm paid by the hour, so we can do this all day if you want* look, which differed from the *I don't have all day to wait for you to get over yourself* look only in the soft curve of her mouth, pulled slightly to the left instead of the right.

Walker shook his head, then pushed himself off the boards, skating back to the center line, trying to figure out where the fuck he went wrong, what the fuck could've happened between them. Was it something he said? Something he did? Something he didn't do?

Things had been weird ever since the hockey game

last week. Not *bad*, just… distant. She'd turned down his next dinner invite, and the only time she'd returned his texts was when they were about skating.

On the ice, when Walker wasn't pissing her off, she was still laughing at his jokes, still rolling her eyes at his attempts at flirting, still giving him shit when he wasn't working as hard as he could be. But ever since she'd talked to McKellen in the suite, it was like a wall of ice had gone up between them. Walker could still see her, still hear her, but he couldn't *feel* her. They hadn't hooked up again, hadn't even kissed after the game. It was like their first day on the ice all over again, only worse. Worse because since that first day, he'd kissed her, tasted her sweet honey, felt her breath on his face as he slid inside her and drove her completely over the edge, and now he knew what he was missing.

It didn't help that they hadn't had any time alone lately. Today was the first session without any visitors—Roscoe and Henny had shown up to the Wednesday and Friday sessions, helping Eva set up more challenging drills, doing their best to encourage him. McKellen had stopped in, too, watching his progress from the players' bench, conferring with Eva during Walker's warm-up laps. Lately, everyone else seemed to know more about his situation than he did. Walker had no idea who would stop in next.

He wished he could blow it off, just forget what had

happened between them and focus on the training. That's where his head should be at. Where his energy should go. But one look at those amber eyes and that uptight little bun, and he was gone. He couldn't concentrate. Couldn't skate. Couldn't do much of anything except go through the motions.

"I asked you a question," Eva said, easily catching up to him. "What's up?"

"Nothing." Walker sniffed. Hard. "I'm good."

"You're *not* good. You've been slipping all week." She consulted her clipboard after all, shaking her head. "I don't understand. You were doing so well, and then... This isn't like you."

"Oh no? Maybe it's *exactly* like me, princess." He skated close, anger and frustration fueling him from that deep, dark place in his soul where all his demons lived. "Maybe all this time, you only *thought* you had me figured out. But you don't know—"

"I know you're afraid."

"Like I said, Eva. You don't know *shit* about me." He nodded toward the exit at the back of the arena. "So there's the door. Don't let it hit you in the pretty little ass on your way out."

God *damn* that woman knew how to hold her own. She didn't back down an inch. Her eyes flashed with fire, her cheeks red.

"Are you finished?" she demanded.

"Are *you*?"

Eva shoved him, sending him sliding backward. She came at him again, grabbing his jersey, shoving against his chest, and Walker let her do it. Let her take control, let her push him as hard and fast as she dared.

The pain he'd been trying to hide all morning was back, shooting through his muscles, curling its gnarly fist around his joints. Suddenly, he welcomed it. Longed for it. He picked up speed on the ice, skating backward as Eva pushed him, the cold wind snapping against his neck. Faster. Faster. The crash at the end would hurt, but he wanted it now. Wanted to hit those boards, wanted to taste the blood in his mouth, see it splattered on the ice, feel the kind of bruising, crushing blow to the gut that would knock the wind right out of him.

But when he finally hit those boards, there was no pain. No blood. No crushing blow.

Only Eva. Beautiful, passionate, infuriating Eva.

He wanted to kiss her. He wanted to hate her. He wanted to stop fighting and just let himself fall.

He settled on yelling at her instead. "Why are you even *here*?"

She flinched at the rage in his voice, but stood her ground, refusing to release his jersey. "I'm here to work. To get you back on the Tempest."

"Bullshit."

"You can do this, Walker. You're close. I don't know

what's going on, but you gotta dig deep. Work harder. Get control of whatever's eating you up inside, because there's no room for it on the ice."

Walker laughed. *Control?*

He used to think he had it figured out. That if he worked hard, showed up, put in his time, everything would be okay. That he'd get to keep playing hockey, keep supporting his family. That he'd find a way to fix his mother, to stop the slow decay of her mind. That he could promise his brothers they'd always be taken care of. That all of those things were within his control, if only he kept up his end of the bargain.

But now he knew the truth. There was no such thing as control. No such thing as certainty. He was tired of pretending otherwise. Tired of letting other people pretend on his behalf.

"Why are you *here*?" he asked again. "Right now. With me."

Eva bristled. "I don't—"

"I've seen you out on the ice before practice. I've watched your clips. You're fucking talented."

"*And*?"

"And you can't tell me coaching kids and hockey fuck-ups was your life's dream. So don't stand there and give me that rah-rah, you-can-do-it, dig-deep, go-for-the-gold bullshit. Because if anyone needs to hear that speech, it's the woman who walked away from—"

"I got pregnant," she said, so soft and defeated he didn't think he'd heard her right. She finally released his shirt and backed off, putting some space between them. Her eyes glazed with tears, and Walker's heart dropped right into his stomach.

Why was he such a dickhead?

"I didn't walk away from anything," she said. "I got pregnant with Gracie. And I made a choice."

Of course. He'd known Gracie's age, known when Eva had stopped competing, but he'd never bothered to do the math and put it together. In fact, after their first few sessions, he'd stopped wondering about what had ended her Olympic career, just glad that it had brought her into his life in the way that it had.

It was only now that he was thinking about it. Using it as a weapon against her, all because he didn't want to deal with his own shit.

"At first I thought I'd go back," she continued. "Train really hard after the baby was born, get back in shape to compete again. But the first time I saw her heartbeat on the ultrasound… I knew that my life was over in the best possible way. From that moment on, it was all about Gracie. I miss competing, hell yeah. But I've never regretted my choice. That girl is my entire world."

She met his eyes again, and Walker realized now that the tears weren't for regret or sadness. They were for joy. They were for love.

His own heart ached, beating into a hollow place inside him where that kind of love had never lived. Had never even visited. Hell, after his father left them, Walker was pretty sure that kind of love didn't even exist.

But deep down, he knew that was just an excuse. One he'd fallen back on his entire life, keeping him just out of harm's way.

And just out of love's.

"Her father..." Eva shook her head, a weariness creeping over her that made Walker want to destroy the man who'd put it there. "We'd been together a few months at that point. Nothing promised, but I... we really liked each other. I assumed he'd at least be decent about the news. I wasn't expecting a proposal, for God's sake. But I thought maybe we'd find a way to make it work."

"It scared him off?"

"Worse." Eva shook her head, almost as if she still couldn't believe it, all these years later. Walker's hands balled into fists at his side. "He tried to talk me into... he didn't... he didn't want me to have the baby, period. Said if I did, he wanted nothing more to do with me, and nothing to do with it. *It*. He actually called her an it."

Walker's gut twisted. Gracie was such an amazing kid. So beautiful, so perfect. *It?* What the fuck kind of royal asshole *was* this guy?

"That man has kept his promise," Eva said. "In the

beginning, I sent him pictures and a little note telling him about how she was doing—just once a year. Nothing crazy." Eva shrugged. "I did it for Gracie. I knew as she got older she might ask about him, might want him in her life at some point, and I thought if he saw her, if I told him about her, he might feel some kind of personal connection. I don't know. It was stupid, I guess."

Walker fought to keep his temper in check, but he was already picturing what this douche bag would look like with a hockey stick shoved up his ass. "Did he ever respond?"

"He only wrote back to one letter—the third and last one I sent. The envelope had her picture, all torn to pieces. There was a note inside, scratched on the back of an old receipt. Like, he couldn't even be bothered to send an actual letter."

"What did he say?"

Eva laughed, but it was bitter and hollow, nothing even close to the real thing. "If you want money, take me to court."

Walker's vision swam with red, his heart pounding so hard it made him dizzy. Through gritted teeth, he said, "Where the fuck is this guy now?"

"Seattle." Eva met his gaze and held it for a long time, not speaking. Walker wondered if she'd regretted telling him the story. If she actually missed the son of a bitch. If she wished things were different, even now.

Eva looked out across the ice, then turned back to him, her eyes totally unguarded, vulnerable in a way he'd never seen them.

In a voice so soft he had to lean in to hear her, Eva said, "He… he plays for the Vipers."

It took Walker a minute to process, even though his insides were already boiling with rage. *Seattle. Vipers.*

Gracie's father, royal asshole, was a fucking NHL player.

One that Walker might even know.

He cupped her chin, his light touch and gentle tone at complete odds with everything inside him. "Eva. What is this guy's—"

"Please." Eva held up her hands, backing away from Walker's touch. "Don't ask his name. I can't. That part of my life is over. He's made his feelings about Gracie clear, and I don't want anything to do with him. My only hope is that Gracie won't either. If that man ever hurt her…" The words faded away.

"How can I kick the guy's ass if I don't even know who he is?"

Eva finally smiled, and Walker felt the anger leaking out of him. "It's the thought that counts," she said.

"Oh, I'm thinking about it. In vivid color. Believe me."

"I know. And I appreciate it." Eva lowered her eyes. When she finally looked up at Walker again, the vulnerability was gone, replaced with the steely determination and grit he'd come to love about her. "I don't quit just because shit gets tough, Walker. But that doesn't mean I don't quit at all. Sometimes you have to walk away from one thing so that you can be strong enough for something else. Something better."

Eva left him with those words as she skated backward toward the center ice, looping into a graceful figure eight. She seemed to be gathering her thoughts, or maybe trying to shake them off.

Walker gave her some space. Besides, he loved watching her skate. Loved the rhythmic swish of her skates on the ice, the fluid arc of her body as she floated across the rink like a feather on the breeze. Every movement was intentional, strong, beautiful. Eva on the ice was art.

For Eva, skating had made her a world champion, but becoming a mother to Gracie had made her even stronger. Better. More complete. Walker felt better knowing that about her, knowing that she'd trusted him enough to share the story.

But for him, hockey would always be his source of strength, his purpose, his meaning. There was no "better thing" waiting for him. He needed to be on the ice with his team. He needed to overcome this obstacle and show up on the other side, stick in hand, ready to play.

He just didn't know how to get there.

When Eva finally returned to him, her smile was wide, those gorgeous amber eyes lit with some new idea that Walker already knew he'd go along with, no matter how crazy, no matter how much he'd rather just scoop her into his arms and kiss her until she couldn't breathe.

For now, he was grateful just to be with her.

Flashing a mischievous grin, she thumbed toward the exit. "Let's get out of here. There's somewhere I've been meaning to take you."

CHAPTER TWENTY-ONE

An hour outside the city limits, on a secluded pond in the middle of Colden farmland, Eva zoomed across the ice, the wind whipping her cheeks, so cold it made her eyes water.

And she was loving every second of it.

She looked over her shoulder, calling out to Walker at the other end of the rink. "How you holding up, forty-six?"

"Just fine, princess." He met her at the center, his nose pink from the cold. She couldn't see his eyes behind the sunglasses, but she felt them watching her, sweeping her face. "Though I'm pretty sure you just Baby-and-Johnny'd me."

Eva laughed. "I'm sorry, did you just... was that a *Dirty Dancing* reference?"

"You know what I'm talking about, *Baby*." He skated

backward, and in a high falsetto, said, "'Let's get out of here. Let's go somewhere and practice the lift. Oh, Johnny, you're so strong and sexy.'"

Eva chased after him. "Okay, first of all, do *not* take Baby and Johnny's names in vain. And secondly, we are *so* not practicing the lift. One or both of us would wind up in the emergency room."

Walker shook his head. "Seriously, have you ever done one of those things? You know, like where the dude grabs the skater by the ankles and spins her around, her head like half a millimeter from hitting that ice and busting open like a melon?"

Walker made a starburst motion with his fingers, and Eva laughed.

"Nice," she said.

"I always thought those women were insane."

Eva shrugged. "No more insane than chasing a little black puck around the ice with a bunch of dudes barreling after your ass." Eva laughed. "Anyway, you're talking about pairs. I don't know if you know this about me, Walker, but I've never been one for group projects."

Walker tossed his head back and laughed, the bright sun glinting off his glasses, the sound carried off by the wind. Eva smiled. She liked it out here. Liked this version of Walker, goofy and unguarded.

Taking a break from the arena was definitely the right call.

"All right, ice princess," he said. "You dragged me out to the middle of nowhere. Let's see some of those world champion moves of yours. Preferably sometime before my eyes freeze."

"What? We're here to see *your* moves, not mine."

Walker held up his hands in mock surrender. "That's cool. If you're scared, I won't push. I just thought— considering all the shit you talk—"

"That reverse psychology stuff never works on me," Eva said, but she was already skating to the other end of the pond, her heart beating with anticipation.

At the far end of the ice, she turned to face Walker, took a deep breath, and pushed off the edge with her toe pick, picking up speed, gliding effortlessly into her backward crossovers. Legs pushing hard, she twirled into a spin, arching backward into a layback, slowly raising her leg. Grabbing the blade of her skate, she lifted higher, up to her hip, to her shoulder, and then all the way up, holding the skate over her head, her leg curving gracefully as the world around her blurred. She could feel it down to her bones; she couldn't have asked for a more perfect Biellmann spin.

Walker cheered and clapped, but she wasn't done yet. She came out of the spin and skated hard, gaining speed and momentum as she lapped the ice. Her lungs burned from the icy air, but it felt so good, so perfect. Everything else melted away as she skated hard toward Walker, *swish-swish*, faster, *swish-swish*, harder, *swish-swish* and she pushed off from the back edge of her skate and leaped, curling into the air in a flawless triple flip.

When she nailed the landing, the only sound she heard was her own heart, thrumming proudly in her ears.

She skated back over to Walker, cutting the blades against the surface and spraying him with ice. "Eat it, puck jockey."

Walker laughed, dusting the snow off his arms. "Oh, princess. I feel so sorry for your future ex-husband."

"Hey! What about your future ex-wife?"

"Maybe they'll meet in a bar," Walker said, "crying into their shot glasses about how awful we are. And then they'll go home together and make out and live happily ever after. All because of us."

"Who knew you were such a romantic?"

For once, the teasing was good-natured, both of them at ease outside the confines of the arena. Eva didn't want to jinx anything, but it was even starting to feel like they might be able to leave behind the tension that had crept up between them after the game. After Eva had stopped returning his sexy text messages. Stopped encouraging his flirty innuendos. Stopped dreaming about him…

Right.

But still, maybe it didn't have to be all or nothing. Maybe, after all this, they could be friends.

The laughter between them finally died down, and Walker took off his sunglasses and looked at her the same way he'd looked at her their first day on the ice, a mixture of respect and desire she couldn't ignore, no matter how hard she tried.

"Okay," Walker said. "That was some seriously amazing shit out there, Eva. No wonder McKellen brought you in. You can fucking *skate*."

Eva closed her eyes. *McKellen*. The name sent a bolt of guilt to her gut, but she dismissed it. Why should she feel guilty for considering a great job offer? It was her life, after all. Hers and Gracie's. Walker didn't have a say in her future, no matter what had happened between them in the past.

Still, she knew she should probably mention it to him. She didn't want there to be any surprises later.

Eva opened her eyes. "Walker, I—"

"Heads up!"

Too late, Eva spotted the blur of white hurtling toward her face. The snowball hit her with a cold, wet sting that left her gasping for air, even as laughter erupted from her mouth.

"Eat *that*, ice princess." Walker sped away, charging fast to the far end of the pond.

"You are *so* going to pay for that." Eva scooped up a handful of snow from the edge and zoomed toward him, waiting until he was in range before launching it at his head. Perfect shot.

"Bull's eye!" she screamed.

For the next hour, they chased each other up and down the rink, sometimes throwing snowballs, sometimes trading hockey and figure skating moves. Eva wasn't sure when the sun faded and the snow started, but it fell on them now in thick white flakes, soft and perfect and beautiful.

Walker was still smiling, relaxed and happy in a way she'd never seen him. Not even after they'd—

Stop thinking about it. You can't go there again.

"I don't know how you do it, Eva," Walker said. "I'm out here freezing my ass off, I can't even feel my face, but I don't care. It's like you make me forget about the pain. Forget that I'm on the brink of losing it all."

"It has nothing to do with me."

"It has *everything* to do with you."

"No way." Eva shook her head, refusing to acknowledge the ripple of emotion his words had sent through her body. "This is what skating for fun feels like. You forgot, okay? All the pressure, all the hard work, the pain... I get it. And maybe I'm helping you tap into that joy again, but it's been there all along. All you need to do is find your way back to it."

"*Now* I'm pretty sure you just Obi-Wan Kenobi'd me."

Eva laughed. "The Force is no joke. Just ask Gracie."

He stared at her a long time, so long she wondered if his lips had frozen shut.

"I'm not going back to the arena," he finally said. "From now on, we work out here. Just us. No pressure."

"We still have to work hard. We've got a month to go, and I have every intention of getting you back on that active roster."

"Work hard, yes. But have fun, too." Walker held out a gloved hand.

Eva took it without hesitation, a slow smile spreading across her face. "You've got yourself a deal, forty-six."

For the rest of the week and into the next, they skipped the arena and the cones and the red and blue lines, working instead on the pond, out under the vast white sky, no walls or lines or boundaries in sight.

Something had unlocked for Walker out here. Eva had never seen him so happy to be on skates. At every session, he was getting stronger, faster, nailing every one of the drills no matter how challenging she'd made them. And the best part was, they were having actual *fun*.

So much fun that she still couldn't bring herself to tell him about McKellen's offer. She hadn't officially accepted it yet, but the man had already made travel arrangements for her and Gracie to visit Minnesota in January. She was looking forward to the trip, to learning more about the facility and the other staff, to checking out what was likely to be her new city.

For the first time in years, things felt like they were looking up in her life.

Eva thought she'd be thrilled to share this with Walker, but every time they got together to practice, she found another reason to hold back. She worried the news would throw him off balance, interfere with his progress on the ice. She worried it would make him feel cheated, that it would damage his relationship with McKellen, that it would serve as a flashing neon sign reminding him that their time together was coming to an end.

Eva was having a hard enough time swallowing that on her own.

"You about ready to call it a day?" Walker skated over to the edge of the pond where Eva had stopped to drink some water. "Looks like a storm's coming in."

Eva looked up, wondering when the sky had turned so dark.

"We leave now," Walker said, "we should beat it back to the city. But it's supposed to hit us good tonight."

The wind picked up then, coating them both with fine crystals of snow from the banks at the north end of the pond. The snow was just starting to fall, heavy flakes

SYLVIA PIERCE

that would stick and freeze on the roads within an hour, making driving a nightmare.

Walker blinked the snow from his lashes. "Where's Gracie today?"

"Christmas shopping with my sister. I should probably just have Marybeth keep her overnight." Eva took out her phone and sent a quick text. Marybeth lived only fifteen minutes from Eva and Gracie's place, but Eva wasn't sure how long it would take her and Walker to get back to Buffalo, and if the storm was as bad as they were calling for, she didn't want her sister driving in it, either.

When Eva looked up at Walker again, he was wearing his wolf's grin, a devilish glint in his eyes she hadn't seen since that night he'd come over for dinner— that night he'd kissed her in the living room, peeling back her dress to expose her naked flesh.

Eva forced herself not to flinch. Not to acknowledge the rush of desire blazing through her.

"So." Walker skated closer, his white breath mingling with hers. "Suddenly you don't have any plans tonight. Suddenly, you're all alone."

"Says you!" She smacked him playfully on the arm and lowered her eyes, unable to take the intensity brewing in his. When she spoke again, her voice felt high and tight. "I happen to be a very busy woman. In demand for all sorts of social engagements."

232

"Come home with me, Eva."

Eva's breath caught, the white puff before her stopping, then starting again. When she finally looked up and met Walker's eyes, she saw the obvious desire in them, mixed with something raw and hopeful that made her ache. They hadn't touched at all since that night at the game—not in the ways that mattered. In the ways that left her skin on fire, her whole body throbbing with need.

Eva had tried to keep him at a distance, tried to put their few stolen, passionate moments behind them so that Walker could focus on training. So that she could focus on saying goodbye.

But when he looked at her that way, the memories of that day on their bench, that day on the suite floor, that night on her sofa... all of them crashed through her, a tumble of heat and desire.

Walker leaned in close, sliding his fingers beneath her chin, his stormy eyes locked on her mouth.

A shiver shook her, head to toe.

"I miss you," he whispered, hot and needy against her lips. Eva didn't—*couldn't*—pull away. "I don't know what the fuck happened."

"I'm sorry," she whispered, closing her eyes. She didn't know what else to say, how to make it right. How to make him stop. How to make him stay.

"I can't stop thinking about you," he said. "About

how it felt to be inside you. About the way you smell." His nose was against the bare skin of her throat, her neck. When he spoke again, his hot breath on her ear made her gasp. "The way your breathing changes when I touch you." He slid his hand down the curve of her waist, down over the soft mound of her ass, making her gasp again. "Yeah, just like that."

Walker's lips brushed against hers, soft and warm in the icy breeze.

"So tell me you don't feel the same way," he whispered. "Tell me you don't miss me. Tell me you don't think of me when you touch yourself at night, remembering all the things we did. Tell me you don't still want me, and I'll back the fuck off for good."

Eva's heartbeat thudded in her ears, her head spinning, her whole body buzzing. She missed him. God, how she missed him. Everything he'd said was true, and touching herself had done nothing to ease the ache between her thighs, her own touch a pale second to Walker's commanding strokes, to his perfect, soft mouth.

Things were getting complicated in ways that she'd promised herself they wouldn't, ways that scared her right down to the bone.

But she couldn't lie to him. Couldn't tell him she hadn't missed him, hadn't been longing for his mouth against her flesh, the scratch of his stubbled chin on the soft skin of her thighs.

"I miss you," she admitted. "Every time I see you."

"Open your eyes," he whispered, and when she did, she saw the hunger there, a mad and desperate heat. He crashed against her mouth, claiming her in a fiercely possessive kiss. When they finally broke apart, she was breathless.

"Come home with me," he said again, his lips puffy from their kiss. Then, with a teasing smile, "I have a steam room. You'll like it."

Eva sighed. There was no use in fighting it. She was a goner. Raising an eyebrow, she said, "I guess a steam room sounds *okay*, but if you really want to impress me, talk to me about hot cocoa. *With* marshmallows."

"Jesus, woman. If I'd known all it would take to get you to come home with me was some hot cocoa, I would've bought a truckload of Swiss Miss weeks ago."

Eva laughed, but cocoa was the last thing on her mind.

Walker Dunn. Naked. In his bed. No coaches, no wingmen, no kids, no dogs, no deadlines, no skates.

No job offers.

No contract expirations.

No future what-ifs.

No fears.

Just the two of them, suspended under the glass in their own perfect snow globe moment, their own eternal Christmas fairytale.

Sliding her gloved fingers around the back of his neck, she pulled him close, whispered against his lips as the snowflakes caught in his eyelashes and disappeared, one by one by one.

"Take me home, forty-six."

CHAPTER TWENTY-TWO

Wearing only a small white towel that left little to the imagination, Walker sat on a slatted wooden bench in front of a wall of gray and black stones, his dark hair curling in the heat as he tried unsuccessfully not to laugh.

"What is so funny?" Eva stood before him in a cloud of steam, hands on hips, her own too-small towel tight around her chest. Drops of water collected in the hollow of her throat, sliding down between her breasts.

"Nothing. It's just... I've had this exact dream basically every night since we met."

Eva slid her hands into his hair, satiny-slick with moisture. "Every night?"

"Every fucking night."

"Then how do you know *this* isn't a dream?" She dropped her towel, her breasts level with his mouth.

Walker groaned, his towel rising from his lap in response. He slid his hands up her legs, back around her ass. "I guess I don't."

Eva pulled him close, brushing her aching nipples across his rough cheek, his lips. His tongue darted out, teasing, but she pulled back, enjoying the game of making him wait. "Well," she said, "since you've been here before, what happens next?"

He tightened his grip on her ass in response, finally capturing her nipple in his mouth, sucking, licking, tugging. Just when Eva thought she'd go numb from his exquisite torture, he moved to the next one, teeth grazing the sensitive skin, sucking her hard and deep, his fingers digging into her flesh.

"This," he said, finally looking up at her, his eyes as dark as the stones behind him. He yanked the towel from around his waist and pulled her close, guiding her into his lap as she wrapped her legs around him. He was rock-hard, hot and slick in the steam, brushing against Eva's aching clit, driving her wild.

She reached for him, fisted him, stroking until he was full and hard and thicker than she'd ever felt him.

Walker ran a hand up her back, tangling in her hair, pulling out the bobby pins and clips she'd used to secure her bun. Her long hair tumbled down her back, and despite the near-suffocating heat in the small room, Eva's skin erupted in goose bumps.

"Slow," he whispered, covering her hand with his, guiding her into a rhythm that made him throb beneath her touch. "Oh, God," he breathed. "That's it." The gentle tone in his voice belied the fire in his eyes, the pulse of his perfect cock in her hand.

He kissed her, sliding his tongue between her lips, his breath as hot as the steam that enveloped them. She released his cock, sliding closer, desperate to feel him inside her. Now.

He rolled on a condom and positioned himself at her entrance, breaking their kiss and looking into her eyes. "You okay, princess?"

Eva closed her eyes and slid her hands over his shoulders, lacing her fingers behind his neck, his hair curling against her skin. There was nothing between them now but sweat and steam and the thinnest layer of fear, still holding her back. Everything Walker did—the touches, the kisses, the whispers, the intense longing looks—made her weak.

It was a beautiful weakness, the kind of weakness born of desire and hope and pleasure and a deep inner fire they both shared, on the ice and off. But it also left her vulnerable.

Eva opened her eyes.

He was so hard for her, so ready for this. His eyes were their darkest, a winter storm at midnight, wild and savage, impossible now to look away from.

SYLVIA PIERCE

Eva took a deep breath, trembling, shuddering, float-
ing. This was no longer a quick fix in the players' box, a
momentary lapse in judgment, a lust-fueled, passionate
tumble on the floor of the suite with half their clothes
still on. This was Eva and Walker alone in his home, just
the two of them, the long hours of the night still ahead.
There would be no going back after this. No changing
her mind.

Every moment they spent together on the ice had
been building to this, no doubt about it. But despite all
that had happened between them, in this moment, with
Walker looking deep into her eyes for her answer, there
was still a chance to back out. To truly call this off—
whatever "this" was—before things got any more
heated.

Eva held her breath, feeling as if she was perched on
the icy edge of a cliff in a snowstorm. She could pull
back, try to find her way back to solid ground.

Or she could take her chances with the jump.

Walker slid his hand along her jaw, cupping her
cheek. "Hey," he whispered, soft as the steam falling on
their skin. "We don't have to—"

She cut him off with a kiss and lifted her hips,
guiding him inside her. He returned her kiss, hotter and
deeper than before, his hips rocking against her, his cock
stretching her wide, filling her completely. She matched
him stroke for stroke, riding him slow, then fast, her

240

hands tangling in his hair, his lips brushing the shell of her ear, and when he whispered her name into her hair, Eva knew she'd been wrong about that cliff in the snowstorm.

Pulling back was not an option. She'd gone over that cliff the very first time she'd seen him on the ice, the very first time she looked into those stormy eyes. She was already falling, hurtling toward the ground with nothing to slow her down.

Best she could hope for now was that he'd be there to catch her at the bottom of the abyss.

Walker buried his face in her hair, sliding deeper inside her, so hard and hot and perfect she could no longer keep quiet.

"Oh my God," she breathed. "That's... you're so... right there!" She was out of her mind with pleasure, losing the last of her fragile grip on reality, the steam swallowing her whole as Walker drove her closer and closer to the edge of bliss. "*Walker!*"

He rolled his hips, hitting her hard, hitting her right. She bit down on his shoulder, digging her nails into his back, the muscles in her abs tightening, her thighs trembling, her whole body wound up and ready to explode.

"Let go, Evangeline," he said. "Just let go."

And in that blissful, glorious moment, she did.

She let go of all of it—her guilt about the job offer, her money woes, her fears about whether Walker felt the same way about her as she felt about him. She let go of feeling small and childish, incompetent in the cruel shadow of her mother. She let go of her self-judgment. Of all the ways she worried she wasn't measuring up as a mother, as a sister, as a friend. She let go of all the ways she'd been holding herself back, all the things she'd been trying to prove, all her old mistakes and the ones she was still to make.

Here, in the arms of the man she'd fallen impossibly in love with, Eva let go.

And when she came, it was in a blinding, white-hot rush, a surge of heat that started at her core and spread outward, electrifying her from head to toe, her whole body trembling as Walker's cock throbbed inside her, and he called her name and pulled her hair and held her so close she couldn't breathe, shuddering against her until they were spent and happy.

When they finally caught their breath, when they finally floated back down to earth and felt the stone and wood digging into their pruned skin, when the steam finally parted between them, Walker brushed the damp hair from her eyes and kissed her.

No, it wasn't the kind of kiss they'd shared that first time, hungry and desirous and urgent.

It was the kind of kiss promises were made of.

CHAPTER TWENTY-THREE

Walker had once thought that Eva skating was the most beautiful thing he'd ever seen, but now he knew better. Eva smiling, her flame-red hair curled against his pillow, her cheeks flush, her eyes dark with desire—all for him —*that* was the most beautiful thing. A hundred, a thousand, a million more nights of Eva in his bed, and he'd never get tired of this view.

"You talk a good game, forty-six," she teased, "but I still haven't gotten my hot cocoa."

He rolled back on top of her, pressing a kiss to her creamy shoulder. "I tried, princess, but someone was too horny to wait for the milk to heat—"

"Don't even try it." Eva rolled her eyes. "You were kissing me under the mistletoe again! What did you expect?"

She teased him with another kiss, the hot, wet press

of her lips making his dick throb. He pulled back, sweeping the hair from her eyes, grateful for the storm that raged outside. The wind howled against the windows, coating the glass in sleet, the entire city already buried under a thick blanket of snow. But in here, the fire roaring at the foot of the bed, Eva stretched out beneath him, everything was warm and soft and fucking perfect.

Walker looked at the angel in his bed and wondered what it would be like to stare into those fiery amber eyes every night, and for once, he didn't want the sun to come up. He wanted the night to last forever.

"What are you thinking about?" she asked, her thumb sliding over his eyebrow. "This one goes straight when you're concentrating."

Walker smiled, but he didn't trust his voice. In a scratchy whisper that felt much more like a confession than an answer, he said, "You're so fucking beautiful it hurts to look at you."

He didn't give her a chance to respond, just crashed down against those lush lips. She gasped, parting her lips, her velvet tongue sliding out to meet his.

He'd been doing his best to keep it in check, but everything inside him was trembling, terrified.

Because for so long, hockey had been his life. His passion. Aside from his family, hockey was the sole reason he bothered getting out of bed in the morning.

But for the first time since he'd put on skates as a kid, he was feeling like there might be room for something else in that stone-cold heart of his.

And that—more than his knee injury and the nightmares from the car wreck and his dead old man and all the other bad shit in his life—scared the hell out of him.

It meant that she had something on him. A weapon.

Whether she realized it or not, Eva Bradshaw had the power to obliterate him, and there wasn't a damn thing Walker could do about it.

He broke their kiss, pulled back again just to look at her.

"Walker," she whispered, cupping his face in her hands. The skin between her brows creased. "Where are you?"

He buried his face in her neck, inhaled her sweet vanilla scent.

"Come back," she said, arching her hips against him, everything about her slow and soft and fucking delicious. Despite the hot mess of his heart, Walker was rock hard for her again, already reaching for another condom on the nightstand.

"I'm here," he finally said, meeting her eyes. Eva arched her back, and Walker slid between her thighs, settling into the spot that was quickly becoming his favorite place in the world. "Right here."

"Yes. Right… God. Right *there*," Eva sighed as Walker

rolled his hips, burying himself deep inside, watching that sexy blush creep up her neck again. Eva ran her hands down his back and he slid his fingers into her hair and kissed the corner of her mouth, remembering that day on the ice when she'd promised to teach him how to skate backward, hard and fast enough to go back in time.

Walker closed his eyes, melting into her.

He didn't want to learn how to go back in time anymore. He just wanted to freeze it.

"Eva, I need to say something." It was burning him up inside, the words clawing their way up his throat, desperate for release. Eva stared into his eyes, unblinking, her own filled with a fragile hope that made his heart pound. "I think I'm... I..." *Just tell her, asshole. Tell her how you feel.*

God, he wanted to. Just three words. But as much as he felt it inside, as much as he looked at her and felt his heart catch fire and knew the whole damn truth of things, he just couldn't make the words come out.

What if she freaked out? What if she turned away? What if she put that ice wall up between them again, locking him out completely?

Or worse, what if she did nothing at all?

Walker could handle losing a game, losing a shot at

the Stanley Cup. He could handle 250-pound gorillas on skates chasing him on the ice with fire in their veins and murder in their eyes. He could handle the bone-crushing, teeth-breaking, blood-spilling falls that came with every game.

Lately, he'd begun to wonder if he might just be strong enough to handle the possibility of never recovering enough to get back on the active roster.

But he knew without a doubt that he could not handle Eva's rejection, no matter how much the words were eating him up inside.

He closed his mouth, shook his head, held his breath.

And in the deathly quiet that followed, Eva's eyes glazed with tears.

"McKellen offered me a job," she blurted out suddenly.

"McKellen… what? Really?" Walker sat up in bed, leaning back against the headboard.

"Full time. Salary, benefits, the whole package," she said, but something in her voice was off.

"That's… a good thing, right? Full time—"

"In Saint Paul."

The bedroom tilted sideways.

"McKellen's flying us out there next month to check things out," she continued. "He's offered to cover my relocation expenses, help us find a place, get Gracie set up at school."

"You're leaving?"

Eva shrugged. "I haven't accepted officially yet."

"*Yet?*" Walker tried to hang his hopes on that word, but his heart was hammering in his chest, his mouth dry.

"It's a good offer, Walker. I'd be crazy to pass it up."

"You're leaving." Now, it wasn't a question. It was a bomb, dropped from the sky and blowing him to bits. He was blindsided.

No, Eva had never promised him forever. Hell, they hadn't even talked about what their relationship was or wasn't, where it would go after their sessions ended. Walker had just figured they'd cross that bridge when they got there.

But now they'd never get there. That bridge was being relocated to another state, and she'd never even thought to mention it—not during their training, all those hours they'd spent together on the ice. Not at the hockey game. Not over chicken finger subs and pizza and wings in her cozy kitchen. And not when he'd held her in his arms, tearing himself apart inside as he struggled to find a way to tell her how he felt about her.

Eva. His ball-busting, fire-eyed, take-no-bullshit, Olympic-medalist skating coach. His ice princess. She was leaving Buffalo. Leaving the Tempest.

Leaving him.

"When... how..." Walker's head was spinning, and he jammed the heels of his hands into his eye sockets, trying to get his bearings. Trying to avoid looking at her. "How did this all come about?"

Eva ran her fingers along his arm, but Walker pulled away. He didn't need her soothing touch. He needed her to tell him that she wasn't taking the job.

"McKellen mentioned it that first day," she said. "But it wasn't a sure thing. We had to see how things went with… well, to see if I'd be a good fit."

The rest of the puzzle pieces slammed into place, and he finally met her eyes. *Him.* They had to see how things went with *him.* To see whether Eva was the kind of coach who could kick his ass and get results. The kind of coach McKellen would want on his staff.

"I was your guinea pig," he said. "Because hell, Eva, if you can fix a fuck-up like me, you must be a goddamn miracle worker. Right?"

"It's not like that, Walker." Eva sat up in bed, level with him now, not even noticing or caring that her bare breasts spilled out over the sheets. Typical Eva, never backing down from a fight. "This is a good opportunity."

"There are other opportunities," he said. "Other… reasons."

She looked at him expectantly, and for a brief instant, he wondered if she wanted him to talk her out of it. Wondered if he even could.

Tell her how you feel.

But he couldn't. The hurt inside him was so unexpected, so raw.

"I'm sorry for not telling you sooner," she said firmly, "but I'm not sorry for making a good career move. For wanting a better life for my daughter."

"You can do that here," he said, but he knew the words were meaningless.

"The opportunity is in Minnesota. I told McKellen I'd consider it, and I have."

Hope flickered once again in his chest. "Are you still considering it, or is this already a done deal for you?"

Eva lowered her eyes, and there was his answer. His final answer.

"But what about our sessions?" Walker asked. "What if I don't make the cut?"

Walker held his breath, and he realized he was waiting for her to reassure him, to insist that of course he'd make the cut. He'd grown to need that from her, and it damn near killed him. He was weak without her. Lost.

Still, he waited for the words. *Don't be ridiculous, forty-six. Of course you'll make it. The team needs you. You're strong. You're kicking ass. Stop worrying.*

But when Eva spoke again, it wasn't with encouragement or promises of things to come. "McKellen already likes what he sees in me. He knows I'm qualified for the job."

Whether you make the cut or not.

Eva didn't say the last part out loud, but she didn't need to. The words hung in the air between them, sharp as knives. His gut ached.

He shoved aside the sheet and blanket and hauled himself out of bed, yanking on a pair of sweats and an old Tempest hoodie. He wanted to toss her ass out, but there was no way he'd send her out in the storm, no matter how pissed he was.

Best he could do was camp out on the couch, get the fuck away from her.

"So it's like that?" she said, words suddenly full of fire. "You're just storming off? We can't even talk about this?"

"You made your decision. Didn't think it was important enough to tell me about, so forgive me if I don't think it's important enough to keep yakking about now."

Her eyes flashed with hurt, but Walker didn't care. Couldn't care. Couldn't spare another thought for her feelings without turning himself inside out in the process, and he was *done* doing that.

In fact, he was done with her completely. On the ice and off.

"You know what, Eva?" he said. "I'll call McKellen in the morning, let him know he can have you now. Far as I'm concerned, we're through."

"What? We still have a few weeks scheduled."

"Sorry. Not interested."

Red rage crept across Eva's chest, up her neck, into her cheeks.

She exploded out of bed, tearing off the blankets and stomping over to meet him, fingers jabbing his chest. "You've got people bending over backward—*I'm* bending over backward—trying to help you get back on the team, and you pull shit like this?"

"Save your self-righteous bullshit, Eva. You weren't helping me. You were helping yourself." He knocked her hand away from his chest. Didn't want her touching him again. "You said it yourself—I was your meal ticket."

"Walker, that was a joke. Give me a break."

"But it wasn't, that's the thing. Because McKellen offered you the job, and you used me to prove yourself." He yanked a pillow and blanket from the closet and slammed the closet door shut, rattling the walls.

"You can't honestly tell me that's what you're pissed about," she said.

"It doesn't matter what I'm pissed about."

"So this is how you deal with your shit? By shutting down and shutting me out?"

"Call it what you want, Eva. I'm done talking."

"Who the hell do you think you are?" There was fire in her eyes, the same he'd seen that first day on the ice. *Every* day on the ice. Every time he pushed her buttons. Every time she pushed his. Only now, the fire wasn't turning him on. It was destroying everything in its path.

He leaned in close, his lips against the shell of her ear, making her shiver. "No one, apparently."

He pulled back just in time to see the heartache in her eyes, his own heart cracking right down the middle. He wanted to see things from her perspective, to be happy for her, to see that this was a good thing. But all he could see was Eva walking out the door, leaving him. Just like his father had left him. Hell, his mother left, too—not on purpose, but the end result was the fucking same.

Everyone Walker loved went away.

He never should've let this happen.

"Don't do this," she whispered, all the fight in her gone. Her eyes glazed with tears, dousing the fire that had burned so hot.

But the damage was already done.

Walker looked at her with all the coldness he could muster, ignoring the gaping wound in his heart, ignoring the voice urging him to drop his shit and crawl right back into bed with her.

Yeah, maybe there was a time Walker would've wanted to talk things out, to find a way to make it work, to compromise. For a little while, Eva had almost made him believe he was still the guy who could open himself up, still the guy who could put his heart on the line no matter the risk.

But all that guy ever got was left behind.

Fuck that guy.

He looked at her once more, then turned away, heading for the door. "Soon as the roads are clear tomorrow, I want you gone."

CHAPTER TWENTY-FOUR

"I don't know how you cook anything in this shoebox of a kitchen, Eva."

Eva's mother Francine set her grocery bags on the counter, wrinkling her nose in distaste.

"I'm pretty resourceful," Eva said cheerfully, biting back the rest. Raging at her mother was all part of the vicious cycle, the negativity her mother thrived on, and Eva was no longer interested in feeding that particular monster.

She had her own monsters to deal with.

Returning her attention to the pot of gravy on the stove, Eva stirred, her thoughts drifting right back to their prison, trapped by images of Walker Dunn storming out of his bedroom. Walker Dunn, his eyes full of hurt and rage as she told him about the job. Walker

Dunn, his house empty and cold when she left the next morning.

In the three days since the fight, she'd tried texting him, tried calling, tried looking for him at the arena, hoping he'd cooled off, hoping they could get back to their sessions. Hoping they could get back to each other.

But it was as if he'd totally vanished from her life, taking her heart right along with him.

She wasn't sure if he'd called McKellen—Eva hadn't heard anything from her future boss—but she couldn't even think about that right now. Her body was going through the motions—Christmas Eve dinner, checking on the turkey, stirring the gravy, sneaking pieces of ham to Bilbo Baggins—but her mind was back in that bedroom, trying to find a way to redo the whole night. A way to get back to Walker.

"An electric range?" Francine's shrill voice yanked Eva back to the moment. Her mother clucked her tongue, making a face as if it was the first time she'd been in the kitchen, the first time she'd made that tired old comment. "Gas cooks much more evenly. But I guess I can make it work—I always do. Did you manage to pick up the whole wheat flour, like I asked?"

"Yes, mother. I did *manage* it." Eva whirled around, brandishing her wooden spoon, but her heart wasn't in it. She was done letting her mother use words like a weapon, done cowering before the woman who'd barely spared them a single hug growing up, the woman who'd done nothing but complain about how inconvenient Eva's skating dreams had made her life. "It's on the second shelf in the cupboard," she said, without heat. Without anything.

She asked Marybeth to take over in the kitchen and headed into the living room where Gracie and Uncle Nate were watching *Christmas Vacation*. The movie was a Christmas Eve tradition she and Marybeth had started years ago, and normally Eva loved watching it, loved cracking up at all the Griswold family antics. But now, even that seemed tainted.

Gracie lit up when she saw her mama, crawling into Eva's lap to snuggle. "Where's Walker?" she asked innocently. "I made him a Yoda gingerbread cookie."

Eva pressed a kiss to the top of her head and sighed, fighting to keep the tears from her eyes. "He can't come today," she said. "He's with his own family."

Her voice broke on the last word. *Family*. For so long, the word had meant something clear to Eva: Marybeth and Nate. Gracie. Bilbo Baggins. They were her family. But over the last couple of weeks, she'd started to think of Walker as family, too.

Then she fucked it all up.

Gracie reached forward, plucking the snow globe

from the end table, giving it a shake. She'd always been fascinated with it, just as Eva had—their fairytale princess dancing over the ice, catching snowflakes on her tongue.

But now it hurt to look at.

Eva closed her eyes. She knew she didn't handle the whole McKellen thing right—knew she should've told Walker sooner, no matter what their off-ice relationship was. And when she finally *did* tell him, she totally botched it. Got defensive, shut down in her own way, just as she'd accused Walker of doing.

She was devastated. That was the only word for it.

Because after years of holding herself back, of refusing to allow herself any kind of closeness or intimacy with a man, of barely even going on dates, she'd opened up her heart and fallen in love with Walker.

And worse, she'd let herself believe, hope, that maybe he felt the same way. That maybe what she and Walker had together was real, despite all the logic and warning signs. That maybe he would want her enough to fight for her, to sit down with her and hold her hand until they figured out a way to make this work. A way that they could both follow their dreams and still come home to each other.

A way to be in love. To be family.

Eva opened her eyes and looked at the snow globe in Gracie's hands, the blue-and-silver snowflakes collecting around the ice skater's feet as Gracie's attention drifted back to the movie. Eva took it and set it back on the table, pushing it behind the lamp, out of sight.

She was too old to believe in fairytales now, even on Christmas.

CHAPTER TWENTY-FIVE

"So basically, you fucked up," Roscoe said.

"*Seriously* fucked up." Henny downed a shot of something that smelled like cherry-flavored paint thinner and slapped Walker on the back.

"Really?" Walker asked. "That's all you've got for me?"

They were sitting at the bar at an otherwise empty Wang's Chinese Buffet, just about the only place open this late on Christmas Eve, helping Walker drown his sorrows. His little brothers were in town for the weekend, but he'd left them with Mom and her friends to wrap presents, and then ducked out, unable to face the holiday merriment of Wellshire Place.

His heart was fucking *shredded*.

It'd been three days since he'd broken up with Eva. Three days since he'd last tasted that sweet kiss, since he'd settled in between her silky thighs. His pillows still smelled like her. Everywhere he looked, he saw her face, that gorgeous red hair, the fiery eyes that had burned right through to his soul.

He wasn't supposed to fall like this. Ever.

"You want us to sugarcoat it, sweetheart?" Henny asked. "You had a good thing with her. And you tossed her ass out over a job offer."

Walker grunted. If only it were that fuckin' simple. But what the hell did he know? He couldn't even remember all the details of their fight, how it'd escalated so quickly. He knew she was taking the job. Knew she hadn't told him about it. Knew he'd said some shitty things. Knew he'd made himself scarce that morning, hanging out in the weight room in the basement until he was sure she'd left.

The words themselves were gone; all that stuck in his memory were the scars they'd left behind and the sick feeling in the pit of his gut that he could've—*should've*—handled it differently.

"She's leaving Buffalo in a few months," he said. "For good. How's that supposed to work?"

"You travel for work all year long. And it's not like you don't have the cash to hop a plane whenever you're in the mood." Henny shook his head. "Find another excuse, man, because Minnesota ain't it."

"Take your time," Roscoe said, signaling the bartender for another round. "We've got all night."

Walker downed the last of his whiskey, then leaned forward on his elbows, hanging his head. Henny was right. Lots of people made the long-distance thing work. And no, Minnesota wasn't the real reason. Distance was an obstacle, not a deal-breaker.

It wasn't even that she'd used him as her meal ticket, that she'd had this secret arrangement with his trainer. He'd totally overreacted to that. After all, it was just business.

It wasn't the job. Yeah, would've been nice if she'd mentioned it earlier. But how could he be mad at her for trying to make her life better? Trying to carve out a little patch of happiness for her and her daughter?

No. The reason he let her go was a lot simpler than any of that.

"Because I'm fucking in love with her," he admitted.

Henny and Roscoe laughed. They actually laughed.

"I'm glad my personal hell amuses you." Walker reached for his fresh whiskey, tossed it back. "Sick bastards."

"You're in love with her," Henny said, "so you broke it off?"

Roscoe held up his shot glass. "Sounds legit."

"Yeah, well..." They had a point. It made no sense. He'd been so ready to bare his feelings, to put himself out there, and then he chickened out. Eva leaving town? That didn't change how he felt. What the fuck was he thinking? That he could just toss her ass out, close the door on that all-too-brief chapter of his life, go back to running drills like they'd never met? "I love her. I don't know what the fuck that makes me, but there it is."

"Well," Roscoe said, "considering it's Christmas Eve, and you're in a crappy Chinese restaurant professing your love to us instead of to your girl, I'd say it makes you a chump."

"Gotta side with Roscoe on this one," Henny said. Then, with a wink, "Despite the fact that we're excellent company any time of year."

"We do light up a room," Roscoe agreed. He turned to Walker, clamped a hand over his shoulder. "Look at it this way. If you—"

"Save it," Walker said. "I'm not in the mood for your Mr. Bright Side, sunshine-up-my-ass bullshit."

Roscoe slammed his glass on the bar. "This isn't the bright side talking here, dickwad. It's the real side. You love her. Get your ass over there and apologize."

"What if she slams the door in my face?"

"So?" Henny said. "What if?"

Walker shook his head. They didn't understand. Hell, *he* didn't even understand—not really. This wasn't hockey, a game with rules and regulations, something you could learn and practice and get really good at.

Walker was so far out of his depth here, so far out into space, he might as well be carrying Gracie's lightsaber.

The thought of Gracie sent a fresh blade through his heart. Damn, he really liked that kid. Even Bilbo Baggins, that slobbering beast, had a place in Walker's heart.

Without a word, Walker nodded goodbye to his friends, then dropped a wad of bills on the bar and headed out on his own. It was almost four in the damn morning, and he was in no condition to drive.

So he put one big boot in front of the other, and he walked.

The air was frigid and still, and overhead, the sky was clear, lit up by the reflection of the streetlights on the snow. The whole city was covered in the stuff, a thick white blanket that reminded Walker of being a kid, sitting by the TV in the morning during a storm, listening for the school closings so he could go to the rink at Delaware Park and skate.

He walked to the park now, alone on an ice white island, his thoughts roiling. Yeah, he owed Eva an apology. She'd at least been trying to reach out since that night, but Walker hadn't even returned her texts.

The wind picked up, blowing snow off the banks that bordered the park. He thought of that first day on the farmer's pond out in Colden, thought of the story Eva had told him earlier about why she'd stopped competing. Her words echoed through his head, so clear now he half expected to turn around and find her standing behind him, hands on her hips, eyes sparkling.

Sometimes you have to walk away from one thing so that you can be strong enough for something else. Something better.

There were lots of things Walker might be able to walk away from—things he might someday *have* to walk away from. But no matter how much he ached inside, no matter what he'd said in anger, Eva Bradshaw wasn't one of them.

More than an apology, Walker owed her the truth. He needed to tell her how he felt about her.

She might slam the door in his face.

Or she might fall into his arms, hold on tight, and never let go.

Steeling himself against the icy air, he pulled his knit hat down over his ears, exited the park, and marched onward through the snow-covered streets toward Eva's neighborhood. Toward his future.

Toward his woman.

CHAPTER TWENTY-SIX

Bilbo Baggins's deep, resounding bark reverberated through the small house, alerting Eva to the man's presence a full minute before the knock came.

"Santa!" Gracie bolted down the stairs, still half-asleep but already keyed up with excitement. The sun wasn't even up yet, and Eva's eyes were puffy from a night of crying, but she couldn't help but laugh at her daughter's Christmas enthusiasm.

At least I've already had my coffee.

"Did Santa wake you up, too?" she asked, tugging on her fuzzy pink slippers. Her face was lined with creases from the sheets, her red hair frizzing out around her head in an adorable halo.

"No, I've been up a while." In truth, she hadn't even gone to bed last night. She couldn't; her dreams and thoughts were no longer hers, all of them taken over by the man who'd stolen her heart.

Eva was already so deep in another daydream about Walker that when Gracie wrenched open the front door and Eva saw him standing on her porch, shivering and red-faced from the bitter cold, she truly thought she was imagining him.

"Walker!" Gracie ran out onto the porch, her slippers leaving tiny footprints on the snow-dusted wood. She hugged Walker without reservation, and when he pulled off his gloves and put a gentle hand on her head, Eva wanted to cry.

He was real. And he was here, standing on her front porch on Christmas morning, his eyes never leaving Eva's.

In his gaze she saw a thousand thoughts, a thousand memories, a thousand things he wanted to say. Things she'd wanted to say, too. Things she'd worried she'd never get the chance to tell him.

She opened her mouth, hoping the words would come, but Walker spoke first.

"Merry Christmas," he said. "I'm in love with you. Can we talk?"

"I fucked up," he said. "Bad. And I'll charter a plane to Minnesota every damn day for a year if you'll just give me a chance to fix this."

Eva pulled her coat tight around her neck, fighting off the shivers wracking her body. She'd left Gracie in the house picking out Christmas CDs, and now she and Walker were outside on the front walkway, snow falling lightly, the houses on her street lighting up one by one as Christmas morning slowly dawned.

"I screwed up, too," she said, but Walker held up his hands.

"Listen. Family's forever, isn't that what they say?" Walker asked. "But for me, it wasn't. My dad was a world-class deadbeat—Mom never had a moment's peace. I couldn't count on him, couldn't count on this idea of family that everyone else seemed to have. So I made hockey my sure thing. And for years, it worked. The ice never let me down. Never lied to me or broke a promise."

Walker sniffed in the cold air, his cheeks and nose red. "When I got hurt... when they said I might never play again..." He closed his eyes, shaking his head as if the memory of that conversation were a living thing, a thing that could still reach out and choke him. But when he opened his eyes and spoke again, he was smiling. "Then you came barreling into my life, ordering me around, pushing me past my limits, and something changed. For the first time since the accident, I started to actually believe I could get my sure thing back. And somehow, in the middle of fighting on the ice, of skating for you, of learning from you, you became another sure thing. I fell in love with you, Eva."

Eva's heart hammered inside her coat, nervous and afraid, but full of hope, too. Full of warmth. And still, beneath all that, full of pain and regret, sadness for Walker, for what she knew was coming next.

"Then the bomb dropped," he said. "You told me about the job, about this great opportunity, but all I heard was, 'Sorry, Walker. I'm leaving. Just like your dad. Just like hockey. Just like everything you ever gave a shit about.'" Walker shoved his hands into his pockets, rocking back on his boot heels. "I shouldn't have put it on you like that, but I did. And I freaked."

"I get it," she said, closing her eyes against a blast of icy wind. Walker stepped forward, blocking her from its path. "And I'm so, so sorry. I wasn't thinking. I should've told you about the job offer right away, but I didn't know how." Eva snuggled deeper inside her coat, looking up at him through lashes wet with tears and snow. "At first, I just didn't want it to interfere with your progress. And then things got... heated... between us, and I worried about what would happen if McKellen found out—if it screwed up your training in any way." She told him about the night at the hockey game, how she'd realized just how much was at stake. "I tried to keep things professional, but I couldn't. Because no matter how much was at stake, no matter how much I kept telling myself to pull back, I... I was falling in love with you, too." Then, in a whisper that made her heart ache, "I didn't mean to hurt you, forty-six."

"I know," he said. "I was a complete tool about it, but I know. The job is important to you, Eva. And it should be. You're fierce as hell. You don't give up. Hell, you made me want to be better. Not just at hockey, but everything. It's what you do. Not just for me, but for Gracie. For your students. For everyone. Of course McKellen wants you on his team—he'd be a fool not to."

The wind died down, the world falling silent around them once again. Eva looked up at the sky, snowflakes drifting lazily toward Earth, catching on her hair, her face, her lips. For a moment everything was so peaceful, she wondered if she'd found her little snow globe after all.

"So what happens now?" she finally asked, lowering her gaze from the sky.

Walker's eyes were startlingly bright. "The first time I watched you skate," he said, "I was a goner. I'm in love with you, princess. I can't promise I won't ever fuck up, only that I won't bail on you. That I won't shut you out again. All I want now is to take care of you and Gracie. To protect you. To be your man. To let you kick my ass whenever I need it." He laughed then, a sound that broke across the snowbound street like chiming silver bells. "I don't care if you're in Buffalo or Minnesota or frozen-ass *Siberia*. I know we can make this work, Eva. Just give me a chance."

Despite the cold, Eva felt a rush of warmth deep inside, enveloping her from head to toe. A smile tugged at her lips as the butterflies returned to her stomach, swirling and buzzing, making her giddy. It had been so long since she'd felt this feeling, she could hardly remember the word for it.

But then it came, settling over her like a blanket.

Hope.

Eva raised a brow. "*Let* me kick your ass? Let's get one thing straight, forty-six. I kick your ass when and how I feel like it."

"I would expect nothing less, princess." He stepped closer, swallowing her up in his strong, solid embrace.

Her body trembled in a way that had nothing to do with the cold.

They might've stayed out there all morning, their toes going numb, snow piling up on their heads, staring at each other like neither one of them could quite believe what had happened. But a voice chimed out from the front porch, loud and clear and completely impatient.

"Mama! Please can I open my presents now, *please*?"

Eva laughed. "Okay, honeybee. Just one more minute."

"Can Walker help me?" Gracie asked, her sweet little face glowing with anticipation.

Eva turned back to Walker, cupping his cold cheek in her hand, stroking her thumb over the rough stubble. "Do you want to come in and warm up?"

"Yeah?" Walker asked.

Eva smiled. "Yeah."

"Are you sure?"

The words hung in the air between them, serious, weighted, and Eva knew he wasn't just asking about helping Gracie with the gifts, about coming inside to shake off the chill.

He was asking about all of it. Them. Their future. Their second chance. Love.

"I'm sure," she said. "Absolutely."

He flashed a smile, and then it was gone, his lips meeting hers in a slow, soft kiss, melting against her mouth like the feathery soft snowflakes landing on her cheeks. And there, in that perfect snow globe moment beneath the twinkling Christmas dawn, Eva Bradshaw handed over her heart.

CHAPTER TWENTY-SEVEN

"Haul ass, forty-six! Move it, move it, move it!" From her spot in the players' box, Eva shouted across the ice, tuning out the thunderous roar of the crowd, the slash of blades and sticks on the rink. Coach Gallagher was watching the goal zone, but with three seconds left in the game, her eyes were on the offense, on her men.

Eva curled her fingers into fists, her heart pounding with adrenaline. *You've got this, boys. Come on, come on!*

Converging at center ice, Walker snagged the puck from the Raptor offense, then passed it to Henny, who passed it to Roscoe, back to Henny, back to Walker, who cradled it like an egg on glass as they rushed toward the goal. Eva leaned forward, her heart about to burst out of her chest as the Raptor defense closed in on her man, but in the millisecond before they collided, Walker nudged the puck back to his right winger, and Henny whacked that baby right into the net.

The lights flashed like sirens, and the final buzzer signaled the end of the game.

Tempest 3, Raptors 2.

It was the third finals win for the Buffalo Tempest. One more win against the Raptors, and the Tempest would take home the Stanley Cup.

The crowd erupted, but Eva wasn't paying attention to them. She and Gallagher ran out onto the rink, sliding into the sea of blue-and-silver jerseys celebrating on the ice.

Walker tore off his helmet and skated right up to her, his stormy gray eyes sparkling, sweat running down his face. He was still trying to catch his breath, but that didn't stop him from planting a kiss on her mouth. Eva squirmed, his playoff beard tickling her lips. The whole team had them.

"I can't wait for you guys to win the Cup so I can finally shave this animal off your face," she teased, scratching it with her fingers.

Walker laughed. "Whatever you say, Coach Bradshaw."

Coach Bradshaw. Five months into the job, and she was still getting used to the title. Still getting used to the fact that she'd found a way to make it happen, found a way to create her dream job right here at home.

On New Year's Day, filled with the hope and energy of new beginnings, Eva had officially turned down McKellen's offer and submitted a proposal to head coach Gallagher and the Tempest team management. One week of brutal negotiations later, she was signing a contract as a special coach, brought on board to teach the hockey boys how to skate.

Walker offered a glowing reference. No one was surprised when he made it back into the rotation later in January, beating two of his old assist records after just six games.

The job hadn't been easy. Just like Walker had been at first, many of the men were resistant to the idea of being trained by a woman. In fact, only Henny and Roscoe welcomed her with open arms. Walker wanted to beat the rest of them into submission, but Eva refused his intervention. She wanted to do this on her own. And now, after working with Gallagher and the other assistant coaches to bring them to the playoffs, Eva was finally starting to feel like a real part of the team. She'd worked her ass off to prove herself, and to get to know each player on an individual basis—his strengths, his weaknesses, his favorite moves—and they were finally accepting her. Trusting her. Respecting her.

Now, the boys swallowed her up in a mosh pit of hugs and high-fives.

Walker kept his hand tight around hers the whole

time, and soon she felt the tug as he pulled her out of the crowd and led her to an empty corner of the ice.

"I'm so proud of you," she said, unable to keep the emotion from her voice. Six months ago, he was in so much pain, struggling just to complete his drills. Now he was leading the team through the finals, the Stanley Cup just one game away.

"It's your fault I'm out here," he said. "You know that, right?"

Eva nodded. "Yep, and you're welcome."

"Still so modest," he teased. His smile faded, and he leaned in close, pressing his forehead to hers and closing his eyes. "Every good thing in my life happened on or because of this ice." Walker tapped it with his skate. "My career. Roscoe and Henny and the other guys. Getting strong again. You and Gracie."

Eva looped her arms around his neck, pressing a soft kiss to his lips.

He pulled away and met her gaze, his eyes full of so much love it almost hurt to look at him. He smiled again, but then the grin turned shy, nervous. Without warning he grabbed her hands and dropped down onto one knee, right there on the ice.

Eva gasped, her eyes blurring with tears.

"I want to spend the rest of my life waking up in your arms. Making love to you. Walking through Delaware Park with you and Gracie and that beast you call a dog."

Laughing, Walker squeezed her hands, pressing his mouth to each of her fingers, smothering them with soft, hot kisses. When he finally pulled away, a diamond-and-sapphire ring glittered on her hand, blue and white and silver like the Tempest. Like the ice. Like the snow in Eva's snow globe dreams. "Evangeline Bradshaw," he said, "will you marry me?"

Eva could hardly breathe.

"Yes," she whispered. "Yes!" She dropped to her knees, hugging him so fiercely that they both tumbled backward onto the rink.

All around them the crowd cheered for the team's win, but there on a perfect little patch of ice, Eva closed her eyes and kissed her fiancé, playoff beard and all, and deep in her heart she knew that all those cheers and whistles were for them.

Thank you for reading NAUGHTY OR ICE! If you loved Walker and Eva, you *definitely* don't want to miss Henny's story. DOWN TO PUCK is a best-friends-to-lovers hockey romance with cameos from all your Buffalo Tempest favorites!

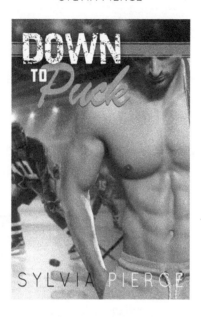

About Down to Puck

The NHL's toughest, sexiest bad boy has only one soft spot—his best friend, Bex. There's nothing he wouldn't do for her, but when things go from friend zone to friends-with-benefits, can their lifelong relationship survive the heat? Find out in DOWN TO PUCK! Grab your copy now.

Read on for an excerpt…

EXCERPT: DOWN TO PUCK

1

Kyle "Henny" Henderson had been yelled at by a lot of women in his life, but there was only one he'd ever really listened to. Only one who'd ever gotten him to say those three little words.

Yeah, I promise.

That was nearly four weeks ago, and he'd stuck by it. Twelve games later, and he hadn't started a single fight on the ice. No major penalties, no injuries, no media shit-storms. February had been a banner fucking month for the Buffalo Tempest right winger—even his agent had complimented his good behavior.

Yeah, well. Looked like *that* happy little streak was coming to an abrupt end tonight.

His best friend Bex would have his ass for it later, but

Henny didn't have a choice. No matter what he'd promised her, he would not—*could* not—let a world class fuckstick like Greg Fellino take cheap shots at his team.

Not without a little payback.

Ignoring the guilt churning in his gut, Henny spit out a mouthful of blood and skated into the fray, popping his mouth guard back into place. He was pretty sure his teeth had survived Fellino's hit, but that wasn't earning the bastard any points in Henny's eyes. Dude was bad news any way you cut it. In five years, he'd already cycled through three different NHL teams, honing the fine art of dirty play. Henny couldn't believe the guy hadn't been booted out of the league.

But, he figured, long as Fellino kept putting points on the board, his team would protect him.

Just like the Tempest protects you.

Henny shook off the thought. He wasn't the one going after innocent players. He was just defending his men. And his teeth.

"You good?" Walker Dunn, starting center for the Tempest, smacked a gloved fist against Henny's shoulder as he skated past.

Henny gave a quick nod, then pivoted on his blades to catch a short pass from his left winger, Roscoe LeGrand. Fellino was on him again like a dog in heat, but Henny saw it coming this time, deking left before tapping the puck back to Roscoe. Fellino tried to drive him against the boards—another late hit the refs totally ignored—but Henny spun away and slid out behind him, passing up a perfectly fine opportunity to charge the sonofabitch.

It was pretty damn magnanimous of him, and he hoped Bex'd seen it. She couldn't make every game—worked a lot of nights managing her mom's pub—but she was here tonight, right behind the glass, shaking her "BRING IT, #19!" sign. Ever since she'd moved back to Buffalo this summer, she'd been making a new sign for every game, all bright colors and glitter. Henny had them all tacked up in his workout room at home.

Girl sure knew how to light a fire under his ass. Always had.

The puck was back in Henny's control again, and after snaking around Miami's grinder, he saw a damn near perfect shot. He pulled back, then smacked that bad boy right between the goalie's skates, bringing the Tempest to a three-two lead.

His eyes immediately cut to Bex. She was on her feet with the rest of the crowd, pumping that sign in the air, wild auburn curls bouncing. Her crazy smile untied a few of the knots in his gut. The last three years in California had done quite a number on her, but if she was smiling like *that*, she was getting better. More every day. And if she was getting better, then maybe—eventually—she'd be okay.

The crowd was jacked tonight, cheering for Henny from one side of the arena to the other. Roscoe slid over and smacked him on the helmet, but over in the box, head coach Gallagher and the rest of the stiffs looked unimpressed.

Again his insides churned, but he shut it down. Fuck 'em. He'd take those silent scowls over another lecture any day of the week.

After the goal, Henny lined up with Dunn and Roscoe for the next face-off, pumped as hell. They were halfway through the third, ten minutes left on the clock. If luck was on his side tonight, they'd score another goal or two, lock in the win, and he'd be done in time to grab a beer and burger with Bex.

Just had to find the right moment to nail Fellino's ass to the wall, and all would be right with the world.

"Let's zip this up, boys," Dunn said, waiting for the puck drop. Soon as it hit the ice, he was on it, dodging Miami's center as he rocketed across the ice. He passed the puck to Roscoe, who shot to Henny, back to Dunn...

And Dunn fell on his ass.

Fucking Fellino. Bastard had tripped him up with his stick.

Dunn was back on his feet in an instant, but he'd lost the puck to Fellino's winger.

Henny waited for the refs to call the penalty, but

when it came to Fellino, apparently the officials were asleep at the wheel.

He chased the action down toward the Tempest goal, where Dimitri Kuznetsov—a.k.a. Kooz—was doing a bang-up job keeping those pricks out of the net. Kooz was tough as shit, but Fellino was relentless, attacking the puck like a rabid animal until he finally knocked it in.

Shit.

Tied with eight minutes left to play, the teams lined up for the face-off. Fellino managed to beat Dunn this time, sweeping the puck down the ice for another shot at Kooz.

Roscoe and Henny forced him into the corner, where the three men duked it out. After their brief scuffle, Roscoe slid out from the tangle of bodies, puck cradled in his stick.

The look in Fellino's eyes was pure rage. He shoved off the boards, charging back toward Roscoe on the hunt for blood. Roscoe tried to pass to Walker, but Fellino got right in there again, swiped the puck from Roscoe's control.

Not tonight, asshole.

Henny was close on Fellino's heels, shadowing him as they barreled down the ice. Soon as they got close to the boards again, Henny saw his opportunity. Grabbing his stick with both hands, he crashed into Fellino and checked his ass.

Damn, that felt good.

The ref's whistle pierced the noise of the crowd and stopped the play.

You have got *to be kidding me.*

"Buffalo penalty, nineteen, Kyle Henderson," the ref announced. "Two minutes for cross-checking."

"Wake the fuck up!" Henny shouted, but there was no point in arguing. These refs had shoved their collective heads up Miami's ass at the start. And no, Henny's hit on Fellino wasn't exactly above board.

Worth it, though.

Brooding in the box, Henny chanced a look to his left, scanning the seats for his best friend. He couldn't see Bex up close from this vantage point, but he felt it right down to his bones—the heavy weight of her disappointment. The worry and sadness in her eyes. He hated that look. Hated being the reason for it.

He shook his head, staring out across the ice to watch the Miami power play. He couldn't even look in Coach Gallagher's direction. He'd get an earful soon enough.

Henny blew out a frustrated breath. Yeah, the boys would always have his back, just like he had theirs. But things hadn't been so hot with the coach and management this season. He'd been warned more times than he could count; every screw-up felt like a nail in the proverbial coffin.

Fuck 'em. If the suits wanted to drop him, he'd make it

easy for them. Retire early. Escape to a tropical island, find some hot little chick in a black bikini to rub suntan lotion on his back.

And so what if he loved Buffalo? Loved his friends and the life he'd built here? If the team didn't want him anymore, he'd bounce, long before they had the chance to do it for him.

You didn't leave Henny. He left *you*. It was a rule to live by, one he'd adopted as a teenager after his parents gave up on his delinquent ass and sent him packing. He had Bex to thank for keeping him off the streets—she'd convinced her mother Laurie to take him in their junior year of high school, and after a brief but rough adjustment period, he finally straightened out. Laurie had even helped him get a hockey scholarship for college, and the rest was pretty much history.

He hated the idea of leaving them, especially now that Bex was back in town. But he wasn't about to stick around where he wasn't wanted. Where he was only bringing everyone down.

What the fuck is wrong with you? Get your head out of your ass.

Henny blinked hard, swigged some water. Out on the ice the guys were holding their own despite his absence. Forty-five seconds left on his penalty. Forty. Thirty-five.

Miami was down near the net again, Kooz and the Tempest defense battling the onslaught. The boys managed to clear the puck away from the net, redirecting everyone back into Miami territory. Kooz took advantage of the break in the action, reaching for the water bottle he'd stashed on top of the net.

Seconds later, the Miami offense was back in the zone with the puck. Out of the tangle of sticks and skates and jerseys, one player shot forward. No puck, no plan, just another dirty-ass move in the works. Henny saw it play out in his mind a half-second before it happened on the ice.

Fellino slammed straight into Kooz.

The hit was hard and high, blew Kooz's helmet clean off. The goalie was down, scrambling like a crab to get back in front of the net, just in time to block Miami's shot.

And once again, Fellino was in the clear. Not an official in sight.

Both Tempest defensemen chased the bastard, but that wasn't enough. Not for Henny.

Ten seconds left on his penalty. The guys on the ice were no more than a smudge of color. He couldn't find the puck, couldn't hear the roar of the fans, couldn't feel anything but the pounding of his heart, the rush of blood and adrenaline coursing through his system.

Six seconds. Five. Four.

Everything narrowed down to this. A single purpose. A mission with only one possible outcome.

Three.

Two.

One.

Henny stepped out of the box.

Then, he fucking *charged*.

He was dimly aware of Roscoe and Walker circling behind him, picking up on his energy, on his intentions, but he pushed harder, faster, speeding away from them.

Never mind the penalties. The fines. The suspensions. He shot across the ice like a missile locked on his target.

Ten feet. Five. Three. BOOM.

He didn't even feel the impact, just heard the brutal clash of equipment, the roar of the bloodthirsty crowd, everyone already out of their seats and gunning for a fight.

Henny was nothing if not a crowd-pleaser.

With Fellino pinned to the boards and momentarily stunned by the hit, Henny tore off his gloves and grabbed a fistful of Fellino's jersey, taking a swing with his free hand. Fist connected with jaw, the force of it splitting the skin over his knuckles. Again. Again. His hand went numb, but still he didn't stop. Not until he felt the bony fingers hooking into his shoulders, yanking him backward.

The official shouted something in his ear, but Henny wasn't done. Far from it. With a surge of new energy he charged back in and took another swing. Another hit, blood trickling down his hand, the crowd roaring, another official zooming toward the fight, his own guys fighting off the other team. He lost his helmet, felt the icy air on his sweat-soaked head only seconds before he saw Fellino's eyes narrow.

Henny tried to pivot, but it was too late. Fellino's gloved fist connected with Henny's jaw, snapping his head back into the glass. His vision swam, then darkened. He slumped down on the ice.

He vaguely heard the penalty calls—a major and a game misconduct. He'd be ejected, sent back to the locker room alone, leaving his team to clean up the mess.

Fellino was slumped on the ice next to him, groaning and bleeding.

Henny managed a pained grin. He'd gotten his man, laid that bastard out on the ice in front of both teams, all the coaches, all the managers, the whole damn stadium, and everyone watching at home. And the best part? Fellino was ejected, too. Fucking *finally*.

He should've felt vindicated.

But there in the black pit of his stomach, the only thing Henny could find was shame. It burned its way up into his throat, into his mouth.

Blood and ash—that was all he tasted.

"Let's go, one-nine." One of the linesmen hauled him up. "On your feet."

As they escorted him off the ice, Henny chanced a

final glance at Bex, bracing himself for her anger but desperate to see her beautiful face anyway. To know that no matter what, she had his back.

But there behind the glass, all he found was an empty seat.

Bex was gone.

Just how much more red-hot trouble is Henny about to unleash? Find out in DOWN TO PUCK! Grab your copy now.

ABOUT THE AUTHOR

Romance author Sylvia Pierce loves writing about kick-ass, headstrong women and the gorgeous alpha guys who never see them coming. She believes that life should be a lot like her favorite books—smoking hot, with happy endings and lots of temptations, twists, and trouble along the way. She lives in the Rocky Mountains of Colorado with a strong, sexy husband who appreciates her devious mind, loves making her laugh, and always keeps her guessing. Like the heroes in her stories, Sylvia's man didn't see her coming... but after twenty-plus years together, he's finally figured out who's boss!

Visit her online at SylviaPierceBooks.com or drop her an email at sylvia@sylviapiercebooks.com.

f facebook.com/sylviapiercebooks
g goodreads.com/SylviaPierce
a amazon.com/author/sylviapierce
BB bookbub.com/authors/sylvia-pierce

9 781948 455015